Contents

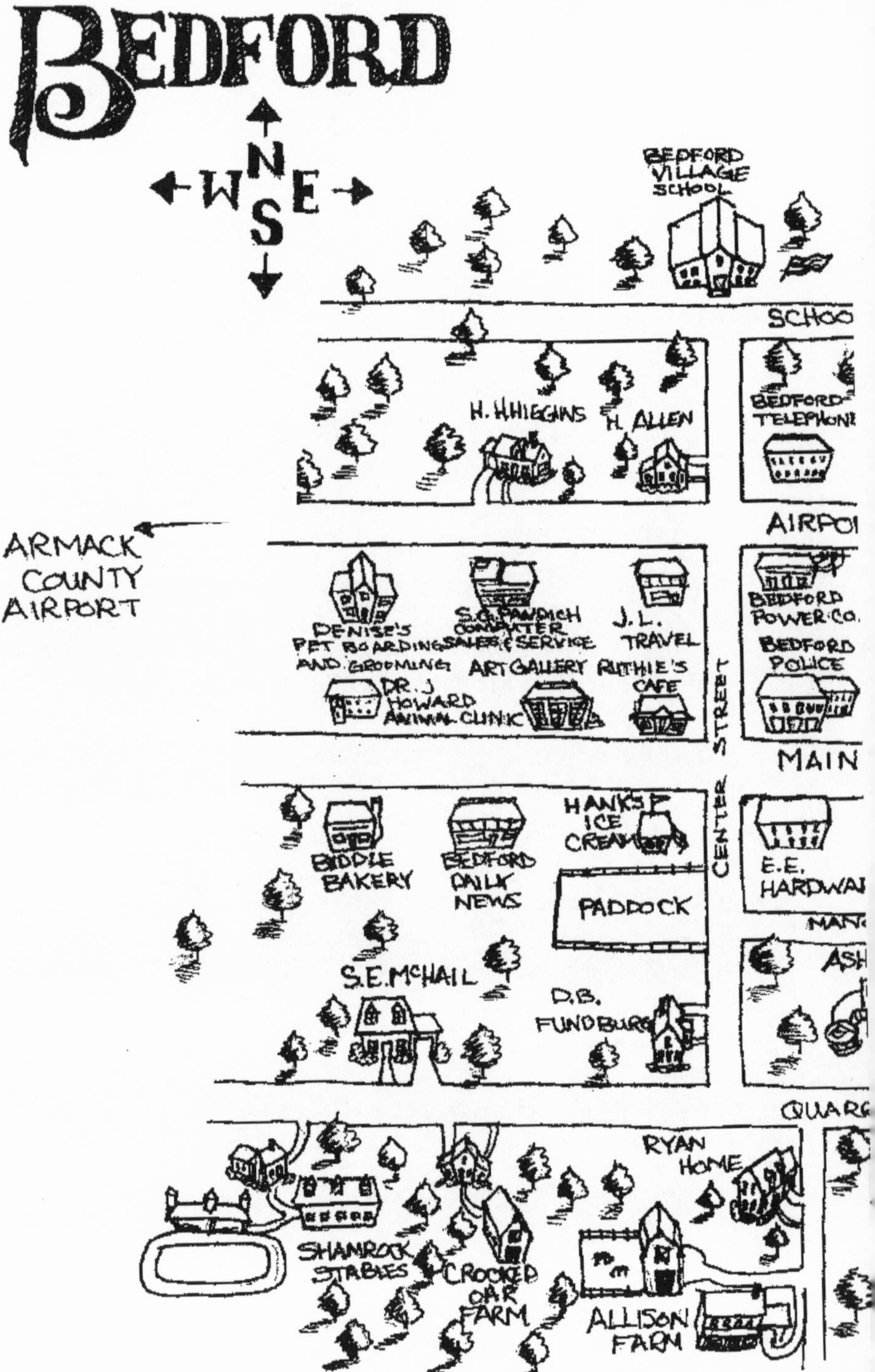
BEDFORD
N
W
E
S
BEDFORD VILLAGE SCHOOL
SCHOO
H. H. HIGGINS
H. ALLEN
BEDFORD TELEPHONE
AIRPO
ARMACK COUNTY AIRPORT
DENISE'S PET BOARDING AND GROOMING
S.G. PANDICH COMPUTER SALES & SERVICE
J.L. TRAVEL
BEDFORD POWER CO.
BEDFORD POLICE
ART GALLERY
RUTHIE'S CAFE
DR. J HOWARD ANIMAL CLINIC
CENTER STREET
MAIN
HANK'S ICE CREAM
BIDDLE BAKERY
BEDFORD DAILY NEWS
PADDOCK
E.E. HARDWA
MAN
ASH
S.E. McHAIL
D.B. FUNDBURG
QUARG
RYAN HOME
SHAMROCK STABLES
CROOKED OAK FARM
ALLISON FARM

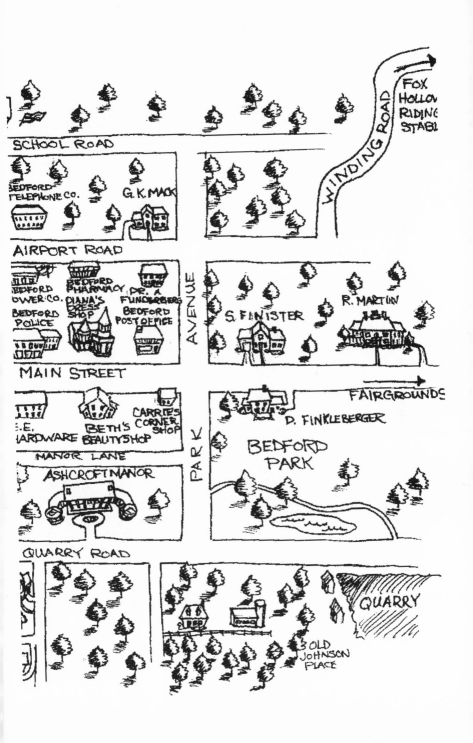

CHAPTER 1

Fast As Lightning

The stallion was black . . . utterly black. The man stood back and studied the colt. It was so simple a child could do it. The problem had worried him during the day and kept him awake at night. And now the answer was right in front of him. The stallion's eyes followed him as the man circled the colt from a safe distance. Shouldn't get too close to a stallion even if he's on crossties. A colt can be testy . . . even on good days.

He glanced up as the stable boy walked out of the tack room. Nodding in the direction of the stallion, he asked, "What's his height? What's he measure?"

"Sixteen hands, two inches," came the boy's reply. "He's 16.2 on the mark."

"Nice," he said with studied indifference. "Perfect," he muttered under his breath, then moved on down the aisle to look at the other horses. He didn't want to appear too interested in the stallion, arouse too much suspicion. Someone might remember his face or that he'd taken an interest in that particular horse.

There were two more pieces of the puzzle to be worked out, then he'd be set. He'd need help. No way around it. Trust was not something he gave away easily. But there was no choice. He had a little money. Finding somebody who needed it shouldn't be a problem. There were always people willing to do things if you paid them enough. But still, it had to be someone who worked close to the horse and knew where everyone was all the time. Someone who didn't like to brag about everything. A tight lip was crucial. He unconsciously pressed his thin lips inward and bit them between his teeth as he continued to think.

Then, he turned around and gazed at the stallion again. A half smile played at his lips. There was only one person who could help him. And that person needed money. But could he count on that one person to keep a tight lip.

*　　*　　*　　*

"You missed a pile of poop over there," quipped a young voice swinging on the stall door. It was the stable owner's grandson, Charlie Myers, who had come to check on their work. It was the fourth time in the last thirty minutes.

His grandfather's yellow Labrador retriever, Toby, had protectively followed him back and forth from the house to the barn and now sat beside a stack of straw across the aisle. Toby was getting progressively warmer from all the running to and fro, and his pink tongue lolled out the side of his mouth.

Amy Jo leaned against her pitchfork and looked at Becky. Her friend hated the word *poop* and Amy Jo was growing a tiny bit weary of Charlie. When she first met him, Charlie seemed like a six-year-old darling with brown hair and eyes, and inch-long lashes. He was still darling, and Toby, Charlie's shadow, was a great barn dog. But the little fellow was suffocatingly in love with these two eleven-year-old girls and adoringly trailed after them everywhere.

Amy Jo was in her usual mischievous mood. "Pile of poop did you say, Charlie?" she began, glancing at Becky as she tried to hide a grin. "Do you mean we have a poop problem? Maybe we need a poop patrol for our poop problem," she ended as Becky shook a clean flake of straw over her partner's head.

"Enough of the "p" word," warned Becky, ready with another flake of straw if the first one didn't straighten her friend out.

"Okay, okay, I quit," laughed Amy Jo, picking straw out of her auburn hair. "Where's your grandpa, Charlie?" asked Amy Jo, turning to the little boy.

Charlie chewed on the end of a piece of straw. He had his small hands in his pockets and leaned against the doorway the way his grandfather did. "He said he'd be here in a minute and I could run along ahead of him," he answered, reaching over to scratch Toby behind the ears.

"That's a great strategy. What do you think, Beck? Maybe we ought to ask him to check on his grandpa," suggested Amy Jo as she moved the offending "p" from the corner. "How much longer are your parents going to be away on vacation?" she asked, feeling a little guilty about playing ping pong with such a sweet little fellow.

"Two more weeks," said Charlie. "I get to spend two more weeks with you, Grandpa, and Toby until they pick me up," he continued, but there was a touch of home-sickness mixed in with excitement.

"Two more weeks," echoed Amy Jo, her blue eyes registering dismay.

The girls had worked at Shamrock Stables for a week now while Huey, the regular stable boy, was away. Huey had been called away suddenly. He said that his grandfather was very ill and he needed to help take care of the family farm. Nobody was exactly sure when he'd return, but the girls figured on being on the job for two or three weeks.

Becky sighed as she watched Charlie pet the Lab. "Well, he only has Toby to keep him company. He doesn't really have much to do, and there's no one around here for him to play with."

"Why do you always have to be so disgustingly understanding?" asked Amy Jo as she fluffed the fresh bedding around the stall.

Becky pushed her dark hair away from her face and ignored Amy Jo's comment. "Look, Charlie," she began, "why don't you trot over to that stack of straw beside Toby and bring us a couple more flakes."

Charlie grabbed the straw and dashed across the aisle before the girls could draw another breath. "Now what can I do?" he asked.

Amy Jo gave her friend a look that said *now you've started something.*

"Well," Becky began as she looked around. Spying the broom in the corner, she grabbed it and handed it to Charlie. "Why don't you sweep the aisle a little until your grandfather gets here."

4

Chewing furiously on his piece of straw, Charlie took the broom and began to sweep. For the first few minutes, Charlie  swept the air more than he cleaned the floor. Frustration and exhaustion set in, but his total devotion to Becky wouldn't allow him to quit. Soon, at least half of the swipes with the broom were hitting the floor. Not that the floor got any cleaner, but it gave the girls a breather and Charlie had something to do.

Amy Jo nodded in admiration. "Brilliant, Beck. I got to hand it to you. That was a stroke of genius."

By the time Freddie Myers came to the barn, Charlie had stirred the dirt the entire length of the aisle. Charlie's little body sagged from fatigue, but he felt like a real part of the team.

Freddie looked at his grandson with pride. "Well, Charlie, I see you're making yourself useful."

"Yep," answered Charlie breathlessly, leaning rather heavily on his broom. "I worked real hard and now I'm done. Did I do a good job, Grandpa?" he asked, looking expectantly at his grandfather.

Freddie's shaggy eyebrows rose in surprise as he looked up and down the aisle. "Oh, you mean you're finished? Well, uh, Charlie," he began, struggling for a positive spin on all his grandson's efforts. "It looks like you plumb wore out that broom with all your sweeping. That's just great, son," he finished and patted his grandson on the shoulder.

The girls trailed after Freddie and his grandson as they headed toward Flash O' Lightning's stall. Even young Charlie recognized that Flash was an extraordinary horse.

The girls stood to the side peeking through the slats. Flash O' Lightning would make the village of Bedford famous. Everyone was talking about the horse that Freddie had brought to Shamrock Stables five days ago. Fast as lightning they said. The stallion was watched during the day, and a newly-installed alarm system protected him through the night.

Freddie shoved his gnarled hands in his pockets. He leaned against the stall door and squinted his eyes at his new racehorse. "Flash will be a great horse," he said, idly chewing on the end of a piece of straw. "He could be worth half a million or more if he wins the race next week, double what I paid for him."

"Half a million dollars," breathed Becky Allison softly to herself.

"Or more if he wins the race," whispered Amy Jo.

Cocking his head to the side, Freddie continued to study the sleek, muscular lines of his three-year-old colt. "And a fine looking horse he is, too. Pure black except for that streak of lightning running down his face," he decided. The free side of his mouth curled into a smile, and his soft, brown eyes twinkled.

"After Flash wins that race, old R. T. Rubble'll eat his words and that's a fact," he gloated. "Rubble said I paid way too much for this horse. We'll see who has the last laugh," he finished with a nervous chuckle.

Toby jumped up on the stall door and looked in through the U-shaped slot where Flash could see the happenings in the barn by sticking his head out. Flash flipped his ears to the front of his well-formed head and flared his nostrils, taking in the scent of his new-found friend. He stepped forward, but before he got

to the stall door, Flash stopped and laid his
ears back.

The sound of footsteps caused everyone to turn around.

CHAPTER 2

Be Careful, Ned

It was Tommy, Freddie's exercise rider, leading a horse he'd just ridden back into the barn. He always acted as though he'd had a fight with somebody. Today his expression looked like he'd been in a real brawl. Tommy only smiled if it was absolutely necessary. It rarely was. The short, feisty jockey nodded at his boss and glared at everyone else.

"Where's Ned?" he demanded. "Flash ought to be saddled and ready for me to ride. I had to waste time running this horse into the barn myself," he continued, then jerked his head in the direction of the bay mare he was leading. "Mandy was good today," he added, anticipating Freddie's question concerning how the mare had worked.

Ned was the groom who tacked up the horses, bathed them after their workout, then returned them to their stalls. He usually met Tommy at the gate leading into the practice track. There, Ned exchanged a fresh horse for the horse Tommy had just ridden.

Freddie tolerated Tommy's impatience because he was a good exercise rider and not many jockeys were willing to live in a small village like Bedford. "Hold your horses, Tommy," chuckled Freddie, amused at his own play on words. "Ned had to run a quick errand for me. He's in the tack room right now getting Flash's tack together. "Just put Mandy's halter on her and put her on crossties for now. Ned'll take care of her as soon as he gets Flash ready for you."

The tack room door open quickly, and a short, wiry man hurried out. Ned crossed the aisle quickly and placed Flash's saddle and bridle over a rack outside the stallion's stall. He gave a brief greeting to Freddie, then opened the stall door. Fitting a halter around the horse's head, Ned led Flash to the crossties in the center of the aisle. He brushed the stallion to a shine with practiced sweeps while the girls stood by wishing that this was part of their job. After placing the saddle pad and saddle squarely on the horse's back, Ned reached under the horse and grabbed the girth. Flash tossed his head and laid his ears back, ready to nip as the girth buckles were tightened.

Tommy placed his hands on his hips. "You're always pinching him with the girth, Ned," he complained. "Take it easy."

The groom spoke without turning his head. "I never pinch him, Tommy," he said in a tired voice. "You know me better than that."

Taking the piece of straw out of his mouth, Freddie sucked in his breath. "Come on guys," he said, scratching behind Toby's ear with his free hand. "Let's just get Flash tacked up in peace. We've got work to do."

The girls exchanged weary glances. Charlie stepped closer to his grandfather.

"Humph," answered the jockey, running his hands around the nose band on the bridle to make sure it wasn't too tight. Satisfied, he walked into the tack room to get a bottle of water.

Ned's cheek muscles stood out as he held back angry words.

Flash tossed his head again and pawed the ground with his right hoof.

"Just be careful, Ned," cautioned Freddie. "Flash is already jumpy."

Toby stepped in front of Flash, lifting his muzzle towards the stallion's lowering head. The tension in Flash's muscles seemed to relax as their noses met. After that the horse stood quietly as Ned finished his work.

"Good buddies," said Charlie, looking up at his grandfather. "That's what those two are, Grandpa, good buddies. Toby makes Flash happy."

"He keeps Flash steady," his grandfather agreed, giving the Lab a pat on the shoulder.

Amy Jo turned toward her friend and raised questioning eyebrows. Becky mouthed the word *ask* and nodded her head towards Freddie. Amy Jo gave her a look that said *you're no help*, then mouthed back, "Why don't *you* ask?"

To which Becky mouthed in return, "*You* always do the asking."

Amy Jo thought for a second and realized that this wasn't getting them anywhere. She took a deep breath and cleared her throat as she turned to Freddie. "Do you ever let people watch your horses get exercised on the track?" she asked.

Freddie nodded his head without taking his eyes off Flash. "Lots of times."

"Even Flash?" Amy Jo finally got to the point.

Freddie turned and looked at the girls. "Sure."

Amy Jo ventured another quick look at Becky, but her friend was busy staring into space. "Well, uh, we only have two more stalls to muck out. Do you think we could take a break and watch Tommy work with Flash O' Lightning?"

Freddie drew himself up and smiled. "It would be my pleasure to show him off to you," he said, lifting his tan hat an inch off his head as he made a slight bow. Then he pointed to the barn entrance with a flick of his hand. "Take yourselves around the side to the practice track. We'll be there in a jiffy, soon as Ned finishes up here." He was about to turn back, but he added. "Take Toby with you, he'll show you the way. Charlie, you can stay with me."

"Thanks a lot, Mr. Myers," said Becky quickly, noticing that Charlie opened his mouth to protest being left behind just as his grandfather placed his hand on his shoulder.

"Yeah, thanks a lot," echoed Amy Jo, excited at the prospect at being able to watch Flash on the track.

Freddie patted Toby's shoulder and said. "Show them the way, Toby."

Toby studied the girls with kindly, golden eyes, then stepped in front of them. He looked back several times as he led them towards the door to make sure they were following close behind. The three rounded the corner in the direction of the track where the girls' ponies, Oreo and Ginger, were grazing in a nearby paddock.

Charlie let the straw slip out of his mouth and looked up at his grandfather. "I want to go, too, Grandpa," he complained.

"I know, Charlie," comforted his grandfather. "But, Mrs. Biddle from the bakery is going to stop by with some choco- late chip cookies for us in a couple of minutes."

"Chocolate chip cookies!" Charlie could hardly contain himself. Before he met Amy Jo and Becky, eat- ing chocolate chip cookies from the Biddle Bakery was the high point of his day.

"Yep, and one of us needs to be at the house to thank her . . . and sample some of them. It makes her happy when she sees somebody enjoying her cookies," Freddie explained. "She can only be away from the bakery for an hour, and it wouldn't seem polite if neither of us were at the house."

"No, sir! It wouldn't be polite at all." Charlie's eyes lit up. "I'll be glad to help you out, Grandpa," he said as he raced towards the house. "Maybe I'd better eat a couple cookies, too. We don't want to seem unfriendly."

Freddie rubbed his hand over his gray grizzled chin. How Charlie's grandmother would have loved that little boy. He shook his head as he turned back and studied Flash's intelligent eyes for a moment. "Flash is a smart horse," he said. "Probably knows it's a special day. We're going to clock him today, Ned. See how fast he can run," Freddie finished, then turned at the sound of the tack room door opening.

Tommy tossed the plastic water bottle into the recycling bin and reached for his hard hat. "What are we doing with Flash today?" he asked as he followed the other two men outside.

"Clocking him today, Tommy," said Freddie as Ned gave the jockey a leg up with arms that were still

lean and strong. "Give him his head, all right?" he continued, his eyes twinkling, but his voice dead serious.

Tommy lifted his legs and slipped his feet into
the stirrups, then adjusted his seat on the saddle. "Okay,
no problem," he answered, meeting his boss's eyes. "I'll
give him his head."

After straightening the stallion's brow band, Ned
raised his eyes to meet Tommy's unblinking stare. Ned
drew his mouth into a tight line, gave Flash a final pat,
and stepped back into the barn to take care of Mandy.

Freddie sighed deeply as he watched his groom
leave, then slowly pulled his belt in another notch. There
were four worn lines on his belt, one for every year since
his wife had died. His hands dropped down and patted
both pockets. "Ah, forgot my stopwatch, Tommy. You
go on ahead, I'll catch up with you in a minute," he said,
then followed Ned into the barn.

Tommy nodded his head and turned the black
horse towards the exercise ring. Rounding the corner he
found the two girls holding their ponies by the lead ropes.
They were standing smack dab in the center of the entrance to the track gazing out into the practice ring with
Toby between them. Flash danced to the side as Tommy
tried to ease the nervous racehorse around them. "You're
in the way," barked Tommy sharply, his slight frame
registering irritation at being held up. This was an
important day and he didn't want any distraction. "Aren't
you girls supposed to be cleaning out stalls now or
something?"

Amy Jo tilted her head back, but only saw the
outline of Tommy against the sun. "We're taking a break,"
she said, shielding her eyes with one hand as she tried

to calm Ginger with the other. Flash O'
Lightning was making the pony nervous.

"Mr. Myers said that we could
come out and watch you exercise Flash O' Lightning,"
explained Becky, placing her hand over Oreo's muzzle.

Tommy frowned his annoyance. "Well, take your
break away from the gate so we can get past you," he
said abruptly, guiding the skittish colt through the
narrow opening as the girls stepped back.

"Sorry," apologized Becky, leading Oreo toward
the fence beside the gate. The mare looked over her
shoulder at the stallion as she plodded after Becky. Twenty
feet away from the gate, Becky tied the lead rope to the
fence allowing enough slack so that her pony could graze.

Amy Jo followed along and hitched Ginger's rope
next to where Oreo was standing. The dusting of auburn
freckles that played across her nose always stood out
when she was angry. At that moment they looked positively scarlet. Lifting her arms away from her sides she
started in. "Why couldn't he just say, 'Excuse me, girls.
Could you just step back a little bit?'" she began, lifting
her eyebrows. "But no-o, he has to say, 'Well, take your
break away from the gate so we can get past you," she
mimicked.

Becky rolled her hazel eyes as she climbed the
fence and balanced herself on the top. "We were in the
way," she said. "Besides, he doesn't care what we think.
We can see better up here anyway," she continued, then
reached behind and gave Oreo an absent pat between
her ears.

Amy Jo hoisted herself up beside Becky, but
whipped around quickly as her chestnut pony began to

15

nibble on her jeans. "Easy with those teeth, Ginger," she warned, rubbing the mare's forehead.

Becky turned in time to see Ginger pull back and drop her head. "Ginger remembers when you used to put carrots in your back pocket," she laughed. "Only you had to quit when she bit into more than the carrot."

Pulling a face, Amy Jo rubbed the area in question. "Oh, I remember that part, all right," she said, clicking her tongue which caused Ginger to lift her head again. Amy Jo's freckles had dimmed. She reached down and tried to smooth her mare's tangled mane. "You could use some grooming yourself, Ginger."

Tommy drew back on the reins and looked toward the barn, resting his left hand on his leg.

The colt's black coat shone in the sunlight; the lightning flash on his forehead was a stark contrast to his dark head. He flicked his tail then backed up. Tommy pulled gently on his right rein and circled the horse to keep him moving forward. They came back to their original position, and the thoroughbred pawed the ground with his right hoof, impatient to begin.

Toby began to whimper. The girls looked behind them, but couldn't see what had caught the Lab's attention. Toby stopped breathing for a second and his ears perked up. Slowly, he stood up on all fours, then he darted full tilt toward the barn.

CHAPTER 3

Hot Diggidy!

Freddie hurried up the dirt path, swinging a stop-watch in one hand, his eyes focused on the ground in front of his feet.

Toby barked once with delight as he neared his master. He jumped up and changed positions all in one motion falling into step at Freddie's side. Tail wagging furiously, Toby looked up at Freddie with adoring eyes.

Freddie reached down and lovingly rubbed the Lab's shoulder with the tips of his fingers. He stopped at the fence near where the girls were sitting, worked the piece of straw to the side of his mouth, and called out instructions. "Back'em up and jog him along the outside fence, Tommy, then turn'em around and bring'em up the front on the inside."

Tommy nodded and turned the horse around.

The girls leaned forward listening to every word of instruction, then exchanged quizzical looks.

Amy Jo opened her mouth to speak, but Becky poked her in the side and motioned for her to be quiet. Amy Jo leaned towards her friend and murmured, "I just want to know what's going on." She moistened her lips and turned to Freddie. "Uh, Mr. Myers, could I just ask you a question?"

Freddie kept his eyes on Flash O' Lightning while he answered. "Just call me Freddie, that's what everybody calls me," he said as he handed his ancient hat to Amy Jo for safekeeping.

"Okay, Mr. I mean Freddie," Amy Jo began, placing the hat on her head. "What I wanted to know is what does 'back him up' and stuff like that mean?"

Freddie nodded his head in rhythm to Flash O' Lightning's hoof beats. "Uh," he began, trying to shift his attention to her request. "Back him up, well, that means to jog him around the track going the wrong way you see. When he gets to that post over there," Freddie continued, tossing a careless hand in the direction of a distant post, "Tommy'll turn'em around and bring'em back near the inside fence. Then, we're gonna clock'em today, too. See if he's made of the stuff I think he's made of . . . gotta be," he finished softly.

Becky looked at the round object Freddie was fingering in his hand. "Does that mean you're going to time him with your stopwatch?" she asked.

Freddie nodded his head. "Soon as Flash O' Lightning jogs back," he said, then shifted his attention back as Tommy pulled up in front. "Take'em over to the first pole there, Tommy, and we'll clock'em."

Tommy nodded and jogged back down the track to the first pole, then steadied his horse. After Freddie signaled with his arm, Tommy leaned forward in the saddle and grabbed the colt's mane as Flash O' Lightning broke away and pounded down the track.

Freddie held up his stopwatch and clicked it on as the two roared past the gate. "Come on, Flash, show me what you can do!" he urged, pounding on the fence with his left fist.

Flash O' Lightning extended his legs, eating up the distance between the poles. The colt's mane fanned out behind him brushing against Tommy's face. Tommy had a whip in his hand, but it was plain to see he'd never have to use it on this horse. Around the backstretch they flew, hugging the inside fence. The stallion's body glistened in the sun; lather patches began to form. For three seconds they couldn't see horse or rider as they passed the blind spot on the backstretch of the track. The three spectators leaned to the side as far as possible until Tommy and Flash shot into view.

The girls reached out with both hands as if they were holding the reins themselves, pushing the horse to go faster as their heels dug into the air.

Beside Becky, Oreo neighed and sidestepped as she watched Flash O' Lightning race towards the finish line.

The whites of Ginger's eyes stood out while the mare pulled back on the lead line.

"Come on, Flash!" Amy Jo screamed, her knees pressing together harder, urging the colt on for the final two poles.

As Flash O' Lightning stormed past the mark on the inside fence, Freddie pressed the stop button and stared bug-eyed at the stopwatch.

Freddie laughed and pounded harder on the fence. "Hot diggidy! He's a winner! I knew it!" he gloated as Becky and Amy Jo jumped down from the fence grinning.

Tommy patted Flash on the neck as he trotted up to where they stood, casting a quick curious glance at the stopwatch in Freddie's hand.

Toby inched forward as the colt drew near. He rested his front paws on the first rail of the fence, then pressed his nose between the rails towards the approaching colt.

Flash O' Lightning breathed out streams of air. He lowered his head, drew his ears forward and sniffed the Lab.

"Good work, Tommy!" Freddie beamed. "Best time yet," he said, eyes shining. "Victory is lookin' a lot sweeter now," he finished.

"Does that mean you'll win the race for sure?" Amy Jo quizzed, reaching out to touch the horse's nose. "Lookin' good, lookin' good," Freddie answered, pressing the *clear* button on his stopwatch. "Got to get'em tattooed first. He should have had his tattoo by now. Don't know why the other owner didn't do it."

Becky looked bewildered at Freddie. "What kind of tattoo?" she asked.

"Oh," Freddie laughed. "It's not like a picture or a word that people tattoo on themselves," he explained. "It's a number you assign to racehorses so you can identify them. Sort of like giving people a social security number or like a credit card number."

Amy Jo nodded. After her detective father had died, her mother was assigned a special number so that she could collect monthly insurance checks. "Where are they going to tattoo him?"

Freddie focused back on the girls. "Ah, you'll see for yourselves day after tomorrow. Let's see this is

Monday, that'll be Wednesday afternoon.
Stick around after you get done with your
work and you can watch," he offered. "A
horse has got to be tattooed in order to
race. They ink a number on the horse's inside upper lip,
never goes away either," he explained. "Some horses look
a lot alike. Tattoo's the way the officials at the racetrack
identify the horse. Got to have that tattoo to race," he
repeated again with a firm nod.

Ned walked up beside the group with a light sheet
to throw over the sweating horse. He stepped over to the
stallion as Tommy slipped down from the saddle and
headed for the barn.

Freddie looked at the colt's heaving sides and
flared nostrils. "Better walk him out a bit more, Ned," he
directed. "He's blowing a little too much to stand still
like that."

"Don't worry, Freddie," said Ned. "I'll walk him
around the track a little before I take him in." Ned
loosened the girth, then threw the sheet over the
stallion's back. After taking the reins in his right hand,
Ned pulled the colt back from Toby and walked down
the track.

Freddie raised his hand in thanks then turned towards the barn.

The girls left their ponies grazing beside the fence
and joined Freddie, one on each side of him with Toby
close behind.

Freddie shoved his stopwatch in his pocket and
shook his head. "Old Rubble'll eat his words for sure
now," he chuckled softly, looking first at one girl, then
at the other.

"What do you mean about Mr. Rubble eating his words?" asked Becky, looking up at him.

Freddie glanced to the east where M. T. Rubble was renting Crooked Oak Farm for a short time. "Old Rubble used to board his racehorses at the racetrack so his trainers could work with them. Used to live near there, too, before he moved next door," he began. "I was a trainer on that track myself. But I always had a hankering to have a place and train horses of my own."

He looked around proudly at the rolling hills and barn he called Shamrock Stables, named in honor of his Irish grandmother. "Rubble told me I couldn't find a winner training away from the racetrack. He laughed at me." Freddie pressed his lips together and shook his head, remembering the past five years. "Until Flash O' Lightning came along, I'd about given up. Borrowed money against the farm to buy Flash, but now everything'll be all right." He shoved his hands in his pockets and gave the girls a thin smile. "Got to win that race next week though," he murmured.

They walked in silence for a moment, then Freddie looked at the girls. "Say, how about a couple of chocolate chip cookies, then you can go back and finish those last two stalls?"

"Chocolate chip cookies!" Amy Jo was ecstatic. "Only my favorite!"

Becky suddenly realized how hungry she was. "That would be great Freddie, thanks."

A half hour later Freddie and the girls walked into the barn brushing the last trace of cookies from their shirts.

Ned looked up from drying off Flash O' Lightning. "I didn't get a chance to watch the colt

24

run," commented the groom "How'd it go?"

Freddie beamed. "Just great, Ned," he said in his soft, melodic voice. "Make sure Flash's cooled down real good before you grain him, all right? Don't want him getting colic on us. Don't need a bad tummy ache."

Ned turned back to the horse. "I worked for you a long time, Freddie," he said, "and never grained a hot horse yet."

Freddie nodded as he reached up and patted his horse on the shoulder. "Right, well, just wanted to check on him before I get started on my paperwork back at the house," he said, then turned to the girls as he was about to leave. " Toby's not barking at you anymore when you get here, is he?"

"No," answered Becky. "He likes us now."

Freddie nodded his head. "Good. I figured he'd get used to you. He barks at anyone he doesn't know—man or beast. He still barks at the vet and farrier, and they've been here every few weeks for years," Freddie explained, then smiled and raised his hat in farewell. "It was a pleasure talking with you. See you in the mornin'."

"See you in the mornin'," they echoed.

Amy Jo folded her arms and leaned against the wall as she watched Ned finish up with the towel and take out a brush. Once again he used short strokes on the horse's sides to bring out the shine. "How do you like taking care of racehorses?" she finally asked.

Ned paused a second from grooming and looked up. "Not as much as I liked riding them," he answered shortly, his voice just barely above a whisper.

The girls stared at each other with raised eyebrows.

"You used to ride racehorses?" asked Becky. "When?"

Ned glanced at the girls with eyes that matched his graying hair. "I used to be the exercise rider for Freddie when we were both at the track . . . before the accident," he explained between brush strokes.

When he didn't explain further, Amy Jo leaned forward and asked, "What accident?"

For a moment Ned was silent, then took a deep breath. "We were clocking a horse at the racetrack, and I was pushing him pretty hard." He shook his head at the memory. "The horse took a bad step and just fell. I went flying over his head and broke my back." Ned's head dropped, and for another moment, he was silent while the girls waited. "I was in the hospital for awhile, then in rehabilitation for a long time where I had to learn to walk all over again. Didn't work for a long time," he continued. "When I came back, Freddie had hired somebody else as exercise rider."

Amy Jo opened her mouth to say something, but closed it again and gave Becky a quick side glance. For a moment, Becky's eyes mirrored Ned's misery, then she slowly pulled her gaze away and stared at the floor.

Ned shrugged his shoulders as he switched to the other side of the colt. "I didn't blame Freddie, still don't. At least he gave me a job." He stopped and looked straight ahead. "But I know I could still ride if he'd just give me the chance . . . no matter what the doctors say."

The sound of crunching gravel made them all turn toward the barn door. It was Tommy, and he was heading straight for the stallion.

Ned stiffened, tossed his brush on top of a bale of straw, and slipped a lead line on Flash's halter. Ned turned the horse around ready to walk him to his stall.

Amy Jo and Becky straightened up and decided they'd better get busy with the remaining two stalls.

As Ned and the colt neared where the girls stood, Amy Jo stepped forward and raised her hand to pat Flash O' Lightning on the shoulder. "You were great, Flash!" she exclaimed.

Tommy slipped between the colt and the girls. "Stay back!" he said curtly. "Flash doesn't like little girls messing with him."

Amy Jo sucked in her breath. "I may be short for my age, but I'm not a little girl and I'm around horses all the time," she exclaimed, her arm still mid-air.

"Why don't you just let her pat him for a second?" suggested Ned. "I've got a hold of the colt."

Tommy's fist tightened as he glared at the other man. "Stay out of it," he said, his voice low and menacing, then he turned back to the girls. "Stick to your ponies, then nobody gets hurt." The two men exchanged another heated glance before Ned turned away and led Flash O' Lightning into his stall.

Amy Jo stepped forward and opened her mouth for a quick come back, but before more angry words could be exchanged, Becky reached out and pulled back on her friend's arm. "Come on, we'll just get into trouble," she said softly. "Let's finish the stalls, then we'll get Oreo and Ginger and ride home."

Amy Jo shook her arm free, exchanged one last look with Tommy, then reluctantly followed Becky.

CHAPTER 4

Midnight Magic

Around the corner the two ponies stood swishing their tails and pawing the ground, impatient for the girls to finish work for the morning. They neighed softly at the sound of the girls' footsteps, one walking, one stomping towards them.

Amy Jo marched up to her chestnut mare and untied the lead, then shoved it and the halter into her saddlebag.

Ginger pranced nervously worried that Amy Jo's anger was aimed at four-legged creatures as well as two-legged.

"It's all right, Ginger," said Amy Jo, reassuringly. As soon as the mare felt confident that her mistress's bad mood was only directed at the two-legged variety, she allowed herself to be led around to the mounting block.

After patting her pony on the shoulder and gathering up her reins, Amy Jo said, "Let's go home, Ginger."

Becky tightened the girth around Oreo, then slipped her foot in the stirrup and pulled herself into the saddle all the while casting side glances at Amy Jo. "At least we got to see Flash O' Lightning run this morning," she reminded her friend.

Amy Jo tossed her bangs out of her eyes as she gave Becky a flashing look. "You're just trying to pacify me, but it won't work. I hope Flash O' Lightning knocks Tommy up against the wall and steps on his foot," she began, her blue eyes reduced to slits in her anger. "All we wanted to do was watch Freddie's horse run. Then, when I tried to give Flash a little pat, Tommy yelled at me and tried to get rid of us." She took another deep breath. "And besides that, he even yelled at Ned."

Becky sighed as she adjusted her hard hat. "I know, I know, but Freddie *owns* the place and *he* said we were welcome to watch anytime," she said, trying to calm down her friend.

Amy Jo took a deep breath and thought about this for a moment as she guided Ginger toward the narrow strip of land on Mr. Rubble's property. Crooked Oak Farm bordered both Shamrock Stables and the Allison Farm where they kept their ponies. "Okay," she finally conceded, more quietly. "I take back what I said about Flash shoving Tommy against the wall," she continued, then pursed her lips and scrunched her eyes mischievously. "Maybe just step on his foot a little bit."

As the girls trotted over the rise of the hill, they saw Mr. Rubble astride his gray gelding, Flint. Binoculars were hung around the older man's neck. He looked up in surprise as though he'd been deep in thought and hadn't heard their approach, then quickly stuffed a small object in his shirt pocket.

Ginger lifted her head and flared her nostrils as she spied the gelding. The horse's scent raced through the pony's data bank where memory of previous odors were filed away. The search came up positive, and

Ginger lowered her head again and approached the gelding calmly.

"Hello, girls," said Mr. Rubble, nodding in their direction, but focusing his pale green eyes on the Shamrock Stable barn. "Watching Flash O' Lightning run this morning, were you?" he asked.

"Yep," said Amy Jo, glancing at his shirt pocket. "Did you see him, too?" she asked, shifting her gaze to his binoculars.

Mr. Rubble fingered the strap on his binoculars, then turned his attention to the girls. "Yes," he admitted. "I was watching, too." He drew his eyebrows together, then continued. "Got a black horse at the racetrack right now myself," he said, shifting in his saddle. "My trainer is working with him. He's about the same size as Flash O' Lightning actually."

Amy Jo tilted her head and looked at him curiously. "Is he faster than Flash O' Lightning?" she asked.

Mr. Rubble pressed his lips together for a moment as he thought about it. "He's fast," he said softly. "Time will tell if he's faster than Flash O' Lightning," he finished, his eyes staring unblinkingly at the barn.

Amy Jo leaned forward in her saddle. "What's his name?" she asked excitedly "How fast is he? Have you clocked him yet?"

Becky groaned inwardly, wishing she was close enough to poke her friend in the side again.

Mr. Rubble's lips drew back in a half smile. "His name's Midnight Magic. We've clocked him, but his speed is a closely-held secret," he said, his eyes twinkled at Amy Jo, then he shifted his weight to slip his binoculars back in their case.

Amy Jo looked over at Becky with a sly smile on her face.

Becky stared back for a tense moment. That look on her friend's face always meant trouble. Finally, in frustration, Becky mouthed the words, "What are you going to do?"

Amy Jo lifted her index finger slightly asking Becky to wait and see.

When Mr. Rubble turned back and gave them his attention, Amy Jo began. "It would be interesting to see which one of the horses is faster, don't you think?" she asked, taking quick note of his reaction.

Mr. Rubble tilted his head to the side then asked. "What did you have in mind?"

"Just thought maybe you might want to bring Midnight Magic down here and challenge Flash to a friendly race, that's all."

She could feel, rather than see, Becky close her eyes and shrivel up beside her. No doubt about it, Becky would give her an earful when they left.

Mr. Rubble stood stock still for a full thirty seconds, then chuckled softly. "An interesting question. I wonder what Freddie would say to that," he remarked. "Yes, indeed, an interesting question," he repeated. "Maybe I'll challenge Freddie to a friendly race . . . just for fun, you understand," he assured them. "Have to give Freddie a call today and see what he says."

A horse race . . . in *Bedford*? Neither girl had ever seen a live horse race in her life.

Few things are more contagious than excitement. "Where will you have the race?" asked Becky, immediately forgetting the lecture she was rehearsing for Amy Jo.

"Shamrock Stables," said Mr.  Rubble. "It's the only place in Bedford with a race track," he reminded her.

"When are you going to pick up Midnight Magic?" asked Amy Jo.

Mr. Rubble lowered his head and concentrated for another thirty seconds, then looked up. "I could pick him up first thing tomorrow morning if my horse trailer didn't have a flat tire," he said, shaking his head.

By now Amy Jo's eyes were positively bulging. "Why don't you borrow one from somebody," she suggested.

Normally, Becky would be cringing at such a bold suggestion, but that was before the history-making race had been suggested. "You could borrow ours," she began helpfully, then realized her van was for ponies. "but it would be too small," she decided.

The corner of Mr. Rubble's mouth turned up ever so slightly. "Thanks, girls, but I think I can borrow one at the track just for a day or so in order to bring Magic down here. In fact, I've been thinking Magic could use a rest here for a few days anyway. I think I'll keep him here until the end of the week . . . do him good."

"So, when do you think you'll have the race?" asked Amy Jo.

Mr. Rubble raised his eyebrows. "Well, suits me to have it Wednesday morning . . . that is if it suits old Freddie," he reminded them.

Amy Jo did some fast thinking. "Well, we'll be at Shamrock Stables working that morning. I guess we could just sort of take a break from mucking out stalls and walk down to the track and just sort of watch you?" It was a question more than a statement.

Mr. Rubble studied the girls for a second. "Why not?" he said. "It's okay with me if it's okay with old Freddie."

Amy Jo leaned forward, her mind was in overdrive. There must be something else she needed to ask him.

Mr. Rubble looked at Amy Jo and decided that this might be a good time to make his escape. "Got things to do girls," he said abruptly. "See you Wednesday morning then." He checked his binoculars' case to make sure it was fastened, buttoned the pocket on his shirt to secure whatever was inside, then turned his gelding around and cantered back to Crooked Oak Farm.

Becky pulled back on her reins to keep Oreo from galloping after the gray gelding, then turned to her friend.

Amy Jo jumped in before her friend could get a good start. "I know, I know," she began quickly. "I shouldn't have pried information out of him and asked all those questions," she continued as they guided their ponies along the paddock fence towards the line of oaks. "But, isn't it too, too exciting for words?"

"Well . . . yes." Pangs of guilt struggled with excitement as Becky formed an answer. "But did you have to ask him how fast his horse was and if he wanted to challenge him to a race with Flash and all that nosey stuff?"

Amy Jo had succeeded in bringing the first horse race ever to the village of Bedford and she was feeling pretty saucy about the whole thing. "Yep, I sure did. And it worked, too, didn't it?" she said, her voice dripping with victory.

Becky gave up. It was hopeless. "Yes," she finally agreed with a grin. "It worked, and it is too, too super exciting!"

As the girls neared the Allison Farm, the ponies picked up the pace. The girls pulled back on their reins slightly and sat more firmly in their saddles to keep them in check.

"Thinking about your nice cozy stall and some fresh water, right, Oreo?" asked Becky, leaning forward to give her pony a quick pat on the neck.

Oreo snorted and nodded her head in response, then quickened her pace fast enough to get home sooner but not so fast that Becky would tighten in on the reins.

After the girls untacked their ponies, brushed them down, and put them in their stalls, they sat side by side on the tack trunk.

Becky sat back and reviewed what had happened at Shamrock Stables that morning, then turned her head and gazed at Amy Jo.

Amy Jo sighed as she rested against the wall. "Okay, I can feel your beady little eyes boring holes into me. I know what you're thinking," she said sheepishly, kicking the tack trunk with her foot. "For the zillionth time I lost my temper. Well, I'm over being mad at Tommy now. No more wishing evil on him."

"We'll just go back tomorrow and act like nothing happened." Becky nodded her head, but her eyes were sparkling. "Then, Wednesday we can see Flash get tattooed after . . ," she continued.

"We watch the race!" Amy Jo finished her sentence.

Becky could hardly contain herself. She lifted the lid on the carrot bin, grabbed a handful, and let herself into Oreo's stall.

The mare grabbed a quick bite and chewed on it while focusing greedily on the other carrots in Becky's hand. The pony shifted her weight leaning towards Becky hoping the carrots would come a little faster.

Amy Jo watched her friend in amusement. Becky was rarely this excited about anything.

In the next stall, Ginger was feeling decidedly perturbed. She snorted as she stepped closer to Oreo's stall. Peering between the slats, she lifted her head and nickered softly as she watched her buddy wolf down all the goodies.

"Okay, Ginger, I hear you," said Amy Jo, snatching some carrots before heading into her pony's stall. She smoothed down the chestnut's unruly mane while the pony chowed down on small chunks of carrots. Amy Jo cleared her throat and peeked at her friend between the slats of the adjoining stalls. "Didn't Mr. Rubble say that he was bringing Midnight Magic to his barn tomorrow?" she asked, knowing full well that he was.

Becky returned her friend's look knowing equally well that this conversation was heading somewhere she didn't want to be. "That's what he said," she returned.

Amy Jo stuffed her hands in her pockets and began to rock back and forth on her paddock boots bumping into Ginger's nose every time she rocked backwards. "So-o-o, why don't we stop and see Midnight Magic on our way home from work?" she suggested.

A battled waged in Becky's mind. "Not a good idea," she finally decided. "I think we've pushed this

36

whole thing as far as we can," she suggested as she wiped her hands on her
jeans and locked the stall door. "We'll see
Magic on Wednesday morning when he races Flash."

Amy Jo's nose wrinkled unhappily, but she knew
that her friend was right. She gave the remaining two
chunks of carrots to Ginger and secured the door as she
left the stall. Her steps lightened as a thought occurred to
her. "You never know," she began, "maybe he'll be outside in the paddock when we ride by Crooked Oak Farm
tomorrow.

CHAPTER 5

Where Was
Flash O' Lightning?

Almost 6:30 and Ginger's still in the paddock, thought Amy Jo in a panic. *The race is supposed to begin in half an hour and I'm not ready yet.*

"I'll grab Ginger and catch up with you," she called to Becky, noting that her friend was nearly tacked up. "Beck always finishes before I do," she muttered to herself. "Maybe I daydream too much." Grabbing some carrots, she scurried toward the paddock door.

Outside a few stubborn drops of dew clung to the grass as rays of sunlight drifted through the trees. Positioning a carrot in both hands, she lifted them high in the air and began to wave them back and forth calling to her pony. "Come on girl, double quick. Need you to hurry today!"

Ginger stopped grazing, lifted her head, and pricked her ears forward, then slowly ambled toward the paddock door. When the mare came within reach, Amy Jo slipped a halter over her head, snapped on a lead line, and gave her a hug.

"You didn't break any records getting here, girl, but at least I didn't have to chase you," she said, holding

39

out the orange bribe for her pony to nibble. "Got to get a move on things this morning, Ginger," she informed her pony as they scooted into the barn. "This is our first horse race in Bedford, so we want you looking good when we get there."

Ginger shook her head and snorted as Amy Jo clipped her halter to cross ties. "Looking good" meant lots of brushing and hoof polishing, more fussing time that was for sure.

Amy Jo picked out the mare's hoofs then quickly brushed the chestnut hair free of grass and dirt while Ginger continued to snort. "Only my pony would roll in the dirt when I'm short on time," she sighed as a cloud of dust rose and settled all around her.

Becky watched in amusement as her friend furiously worked her way to the mare's hindquarters. "You don't have to wear yourself out," she began. "It only takes five minutes to get there."

Amy Jo stopped and rested her arm over Ginger's back. "You're right," she said, catching her breath, then sneezed as she dusted off the front of her shirt.

In silence, they finished tacking up. Their ponies sensed the urgency the girls felt and did everything they could to delay departure. First, Oreo blew air into her stomach so that Becky couldn't pull the girth tightly enough. Then, Ginger wouldn't open her mouth to accept the bit. Outside the girls had to walk them around the mounting block twice because the mares refused to stand close enough to the steps to be mounted. Talk about stress! Finally, both girls were seated on their ponies and turned towards Shamrock Stables. Five minutes later they were trotting between the gateposts at the entrance to Freddie's farm.

Even from the beginning of the lane, they could see the horse van parked in front of the barn. Mr. Rubble stood beside the van with a black horse . . . no lightning streak on his forehead. They could see that even from 100 feet away. It must be Midnight Magic. He had his racing saddle on and looked ready to go. They reined in their ponies and settled into their saddles. They weren't late. But where was Flash O' Lightning? He must still be in the barn.

Toby was beside the horse van sniffing at the wheels, but every few seconds he'd stop sniffing and whimper.

Freddie came out of the barn followed by a downcast Charlie. When Freddie saw the girls approaching the barn, he lengthened his stride in their direction. His hat was in one hand and a piece of straw was in the other.

Charlie hurried after his grandfather with Toby trotting along at the little boy's heels. Boy and dog stood close beside the older man looking up at the girls. For the first time since they'd met him, the little guy was strangely silent.

Freddie slipped his hat on his head and pulled it down roughly over his brow. "Look, girls," he began. A single drop of perspiration traced a crease down the side of his face. "Something's come up. What I mean is . . . I won't need you today," he continued. Freddie's face was pale and drawn. "Maybe won't need you for a day or two." He thought for a second as he took in a couple of shallow breaths, then added, "I'll let you know," he finished, then retraced his steps back to the barn.

Toby glanced up at the boy which usually sent his tail to wagging. Today, the Lab just stood there and stared at the little boy.

The girls looked at each other dumbfounded, then turned to Charlie and finally at Toby. Somebody must have died. Charlie's parents?

Amy Jo leaned forward in her saddle unsure of even what to ask. She would have dismounted and placed her arm around the little fellow, but Freddie had asked them to leave and they didn't want to risk upsetting him even more than he already was. "Charlie," she began, "what's the matter? What happened?"

Charlie opened his mouth, then closed it. A giant tear was in each eye, but hadn't spilled over yet. His lips trembled, and he peered at Toby who was nosing his hand. As he looked down at the Lab, the tears automatically slid out of his eyes and down his face.

Becky nudged her pony forward so that she could place her hand on the little boy's head. "Charlie," she said softly, stroking the top of his hair, "we want to help you. Is there something we can do?"

Charlie looked up as his little body shuddered. He shook his head as more tears formed in his eyes. Grabbing Toby by the collar, Charlie turned around and walked back to where his grandfather stood.

The girls remained long enough to see Mr. Rubble walk Midnight Magic back onto the horse van and close its door.

CHAPTER 6

Mysterious Disappearance

Amy Jo stared at the morning newspaper in disbelief as she swallowed her last bit of toast. "I don't believe it!" she cried.

"Don't believe what?" asked Mrs. Ryan looking up from her desk.

"What I just read in the paper!" replied Amy Jo as she raced out of the house to grab her bike.

Amy Jo skidded to a stop on her bicycle, tossed it against the fence, and raced into the barn. "Did you read the morning paper yet?" she asked wide-eyed, then hopped on top of the tack trunk and shook the newspaper open to the front page.

Becky looked up from cleaning tack. "We delivered the newspaper for two weeks this summer, but I didn't think you ever read it," she answered as she eased herself onto the tack trunk beside her friend.

Amy Jo gave Becky a wilting look before replying. "Sherlock Holmes always read the newspaper and so do I," she said defensively. "How are you going to find out stuff if you don't read the newspaper? Anyway, look at this," she continued, holding the front page up for Becky to see.

Bedford Daily News

Thursday August 2

Police Investigate Mysterious Disappearance of Horse

Sometime between midnight and 6:00 a.m. early Wednesday morning a valuable racehorse was stolen from Shamrock Stables. Mr. Myers, the owner, was stunned and grieved over the theft. No charges have been filed, but according to Officer Higgins of the Bedford Police Department, evidence has been discovered that may lead to an early arrest.

Shocked, Becky turned to meet her friend's steady gaze.

"I know," said Amy Jo, nodding her head, "nobody died or anything! Everyone was upset because one of the horses was stolen!"

The grief the Myers' family felt showed on Becky's face. "But why didn't they just tell us?" she cried. Amy Jo looked completely confused. "And here I am the best detective in the village and I'm kept totally in the dark. And now the trail for finding Flash is getting colder by the minute."

Becky read the newspaper article again. "But it doesn't say that the stolen horse is Flash O' Lightning," she commented to her friend. "Maybe one of the other horses got stolen."

Amy Jo gave her a doubtful look. "I don't think Freddie would grieve over any other horse except Flash,"

she said, slipping down off the tack
trunk.

Becky nodded her head in agreement. "And everyone was definitely grieving yesterday morning. Even Toby was whimpering."

Amy Jo had already moved into Ginger's stall and slipped the halter over the pony's head. "Let's hurry and get our work done so we can ride into town and find out more about it."

Becky filled her pony's water bucket as she called over her shoulder. "Dad ordered something from Double E Hardware Store and he asked me to pick it up this morning, so I was headed into town anyway."

Amy Jo voiced her approval. "Good, Uncle Eugene's the first person I want to talk to, and that'll give us a chance to ask him if he knows anything about it."

Becky looked up from spreading clean straw over Oreo's stall. "What makes you think he'll know more about it than anyone else?" she asked.

"Tommy lives in the apartment over his store," answered Amy Jo with a knowing look.

Becky let her breath out slowly between rounded lips.

*   *   *   *

The girls entered the village the back way and turned the ponies out in the paddock behind Hank's Ice Cream Store.

Inside E.E. Hardware, Uncle Eugene stood behind the counter wearing his "E.E. Hardware Store" apron.

47

He pressed his lips together and raised his eyebrows as he peered through bifocal lenses at some bills spread out before him. He ran his finger slowly down the list checking each item carefully against what he'd ordered from the manufacturer.

Uncle Eugene looked up when the bell attached to the top of the door jingled. Amy Jo and Becky waved as they closed the door and made their way down the rows of saws, hammers, and nails on their way to the counter.

"Morning, girls," said Uncle Eugene, smiling warmly as he pushed his work aside. He bent down, dug out a small package from a lower shelf, then handed it to Becky. "Tell your dad I'll put this on his bill. He can settle up next time he stops by . . . no hurry."

"Thanks, Uncle Eugene," said Becky, tucking the package under her arm.

Amy Jo took a deep breath, ready to pour out all the news when the bell over the door jingled again.

Uncle Eugene glanced over their heads, a look of surprise registering in his blue-green eyes.

The girls turned in time to see Miss Ruthie, owner of Ruthie's Cafe, walk through the front door shaking a newspaper in front of her as she moved towards the counter.

"Don't usually see you this time of day, Ruthie," Uncle Eugene began. "Anything wrong?"

Miss Ruthie dabbed at her eyes with a handkerchief that had the letter "R" embroidered in the corner. Smoothing back a gray curl from her forehead, she handed the newspaper to Uncle Eugene without a word.

"Poor Freddie," she said to Uncle Eugene, smiling a quick hello to the girls. "We've been friends for . . .

well, for years. Actually, Freddie was my brother John's friend. Of course, they were much older than I."

Uncle Eugene stepped out from behind the counter and adjusted his glasses to read. "What's all this?" he asked, tilting his head back slightly so that his eyes caught the right angle for his bifocals.

"The newspaper was a bit late, and then I got busy at the cafe," Miss Ruthie began. "Usually I hear all the news from one of my customers anyway . . . seems like they just can't wait to tell me the latest gossip whether I want to hear it or not. But, today when something like this happens to poor Freddie and nobody said a word."

Poor Miss Ruthie was beside herself worrying about her childhood friend. "I didn't have a chance to look at the front page until now." She shook her head and dabbed her eyes again. "Just when it looked like everything was turning around for Freddie, too," she sighed.

Uncle Eugene began to mutter out loud. ". . . But according to Officer Higgins of the Bedford Police Department, evidence has been discovered that may lead to an early arrest." His eyes widened as he stroked his chin with his right hand. "My, my, my," he said softly, shaking his head, "and in our little neck of the woods, too."

The girls exchanged anxious looks. "Do you know which horse got stolen?" asked Amy Jo, trying to squeeze into their line of vision.

Miss Ruthie looked down at the girls hovering at their elbows. "Oh, sorry, girls," she said, opening the paper wider so that they could see it.

"Thanks, but we've already read it," Amy Jo explained.

Becky's mouth felt dry as she looked first at Uncle Eugene then at Miss Ruthie. "Do you think it was Flash O' Lightning?" she asked.

Miss Ruthie pressed her lips together and nodded. "The newspaper doesn't say which horse was stolen, but as I was reading the headline one of my customers at the cafe said it was Flash O' Lightning."

Uncle Eugene thought for a second. "Strange they didn't put the name of the horse in the paper," he finally said.

The other three nodded their heads in agreement.

Amy Jo folded her arms. "I wonder what evidence was found that may lead to an early arrest?" she asked.

Uncle Eugene exchanged glances with Miss Ruthie, the same unspoken question on their lips, but instead he said, "Freddie worked so hard to build up Shamrock Stables." He shook his head again.

"I just don't know if he can keep his barn going now," Miss Ruthie added, concern etched in her voice. "He took out that big mortgage against the farm to buy the horse . . .," her voice drifted off.

The quiet in the hardware store was broken by the sound of creaking stairs outside leading to the apartment overhead. All four heads swung towards the window. Officer Higgins was climbing the steps to Tommy's apartment clutching a white piece of paper in his left hand.

CHAPTER 7

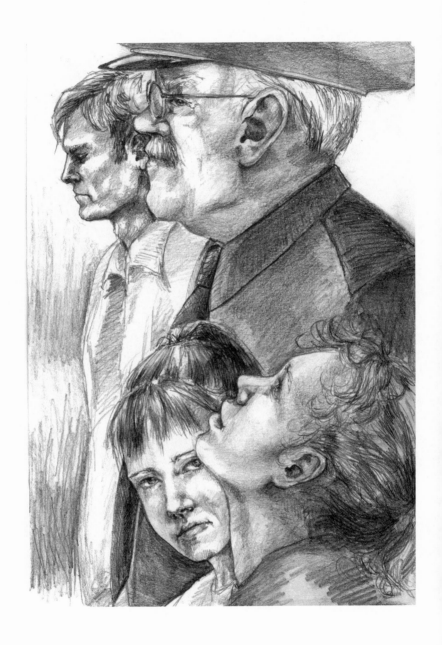

A Formal Charge

Uncle Eugene ran a steady hand over his graying hair, then stepped around a display of flashlights on his way to the door, Miss Ruthie and the girls hard on his heels.

They joined a small crowd that had also spied the officer walking up the steps. "Don't you rent that apartment to . . .?" Miss Ruthie stopped as she looked at Uncle Eugene with a questioning look.

He drew in his breath as his eyes trailed up the outside stairs. "Tommy," he answered briefly.

I knew it, Amy Jo's knowing look said to Becky.

The door opened to the upstairs apartment, and Officer Higgins stepped out leading Tommy who was handcuffed at the wrists.

Officer Higgins adjusted his glasses as he saw the nosey villagers at the bottom of the steps, then sighed wearily as the nosiest one of all pushed her way to the front of the pack. "Step aside," he directed as they reached the sidewalk. Reaching out with his short, muscular arm, he parted the people gathered to witness this rare event.

As they cleared the edge of the crowd, Amy Jo fell into step with the officer with Becky trailing along behind.

Amy Jo's ponytail swung back and forth as she kept pace with the two men on the sidewalk. "What are you going to charge Tommy with?" she asked, as she stared up at the officer who was only a head and a half taller than she was.

Tommy leaned forward slightly to see who was speaking. "Not you again," he said, his lips forming a thin line.

Amy Jo smiled sweetly into Tommy's scowling face. "Yep, just little ol' me," she answered.

Officer Higgins gave Amy Jo a look that said, *Not now*, but answered, "A little young to be acting as his lawyer, wouldn't you say?"

Amy Jo ignored the officer's remark and repeated the question. "So, what are you charging Tommy with?"

Officer Higgins sighed again, but for a different reason. "Tommy will be charged within six hours by the local judge just like everybody else," he said with a grimace. "There'll be more about it in the papers tomorrow morning, Amy Jo."

Amy Jo looked back at Becky. "The judge will have to set bail," she informed her partner. "I wonder if Tommy can come up with the money to get out of jail," she added, shaking her head. "I doubt if anyone can help him. He'll probably end up at the county prison until the trial."

"Comforting little kid, ain't she?" Tommy said to the officer.

Becky caught a quick look at Tommy's frowning profile then turned to Amy Jo. "How do you know all that stuff?" she asked.

Amy Jo drew her eyebrows together. "My Dad used to talk about police business at home," she answered quietly. Then, realizing that the officer and Tommy had gained two steps while she'd turned away, she lengthened her stride.

Amy Jo checked her watch as she fell into step with the two men. "Six hours puts it about four o'clock," she stated. "Think you'll have a formal charge pulled together by then?"

Officer Higgins looked both ways before stepping off the curb and onto the street with his prisoner. "I've been a police officer for twenty-five years. Trust me, Tommy will be charged no later than four o'clock this afternoon," he assured her.

Amy Jo fired the next question. "He doesn't have much money," she explained, following them across the street. "Do you think he'll be able to post bail so he can get out of jail?"

"Couldn't tell you," he replied in exasperation.

Amy Jo posed her last question. "Probably end up at the county prison, wouldn't you say?"

Officer Higgins pulled Tommy to a stop outside the police station. Placing his free hand on his hip, he turned to look down at Amy Jo, his blue eyes unblinking and stern. "Right now, I am taking Tommy into the police station, and when the door closes, I want you to be on this side of it. Is that clear?"

Amy Jo swallowed hard, but knew when she'd met defeat. "Yes, sir," she said.

Officer Higgins nodded his head, then directed his prisoner through the door, closing it firmly behind them.

Amy Jo stuffed her hands in her pockets as she stepped onto the street again. "Seemed a little fussy today," she said, drawing her lips together.

Becky rolled her eyes, but made no comment as she took in the set of Amy Jo's determined jaw.

Miss Ruthie and Uncle Eugene sat side by side on a bench in front of his store as the girls stopped in front of them.

Amy Jo looked at Uncle Eugene and tilted her head to the side. "Tommy lives in the apartment over your hardware store. Do you really think he'd do something like this?" she asked.

Uncle Eugene blinked his eyes a few times as he stroked his chin. "Wouldn't have thought it," he said slowly. "Stayed to himself, but seemed like a nice enough young man."

Miss Ruthie tapped the arm of the bench, then added. "If Tommy's charged with horse stealing, I doubt if he'll be able to afford a lawyer. They'll have to appoint someone to defend him. No one around here does that sort of thing, guess they'll have to go to the county seat."

Amy Jo chewed on her lower lip as she stared at the door of the police station, then turned back to Uncle Eugene. "I still wonder what the evidence was that they talked about in the newspaper."

Uncle Eugene shook his head. "Don't know what it could be," he thought out loud. "Guess we'll find out in the paper tomorrow," he finished.

Becky studied Amy Jo curiously. "Let's go get the ponies," she said suddenly. "I want to leave."

Amy Jo turned her head quickly and looked at Becky. "Good idea," she agreed. "See you later, Uncle

Eugene. Bye, Miss Ruthie," she called as
the girls stepped into the alley leading
to the paddock.

"Bye," Becky echoed quickly over her shoulder.

Uncle Eugene and Miss Ruthie settled back to
their newspaper, but returned an absent, "Bye, girls,"
nonetheless.

Becky gave Amy Jo a sideward glance as they
hurried to the paddock. "I know what you're thinking,"
she began, her eyes narrowing. "And I can tell you this
. . . I don't like investigating places where dangerous
things happen."

Amy Jo shrugged her shoulders as if she had no
idea what her friend was suggesting. "I don't have the
vaguest idea what you're talking about," she said.

"Huh!" Becky answered. "I heard that little
comment you made to Uncle Eugene about the evidence."

Amy Jo raised her hands, palms up. "All I said
was I wonder what the evidence is, and you go ballistic."

"I am not going ballistic!" said Becky, raising
her voice. "But I just know we're going to end up at
Shamrock Stables asking a bunch of questions and
offering to help solve the case!"

Amy Jo stopped in her tracks and turned to face
her friend. She placed her hand on Becky's shoulder and
looked deeply into her friend's hazel eyes. "Beck," she
said calmly, "that poor man's probably desperate for an-
swers, and I think it's wonderful of you to want to
give him a hand."

Becky brushed Amy Jo's hand off her shoulder
and resumed walking toward the paddock again. "I just

knew it," she fumed. "We're going out there, aren't we?" she finished.

Amy Jo's eyes twinkled, but she managed to keep a straight face. "Hey, it was your idea," she said. "I'm just tagging along, that's all."

Becky's eyes took on a look of defiance. "What makes you think there's anything we can do to help Freddie, or that he wants us out there in the first place?" she asked.

Amy Jo looked at her friend in surprise. "Freddie might not even know Tommy's been arrested. Maybe he'll want to help get him out of jail or something."

"How could he help him?" asked Becky, equally surprised. "He doesn't have any extra money. Anyway, I thought you didn't like Tommy?"

"I don't," said Amy Jo, straightening her shoulders, "but, now that he's been arrested he's part of the case."

Becky lifted both hands in front of her. "Well, Tommy's been arrested for stealing a horse, so I don't know what we can do about it."

Amy Jo let out a short laugh. "We haven't started working on the case yet; we might be able to do a lot," she said.

As they neared the paddock, both ponies jostled for space at the gate. Each wanted to be the first to get a piece of candy if it were offered.

Amy Jo reached in her pocket and pulled out a Jolly Rancher. Then, rubbing Ginger between the ears, Amy Jo placed the candy in the middle of her hand and offered it to her pony.

Becky sighed as she pulled on her hard hat. "What can we possibly find? The police have already been

there. No one's going to tell us anything,"
she said, picking up the saddle and placing
it on Oreo's back.

Oreo turned her head around to look at Becky.
Where's mine? her eyes asked.

Becky fished into her friend's pocket and drew
out a watermelon-flavored Jolly Rancher, then popped it
into the mare's mouth.

Ginger nudged Amy Jo's arm as she watched Oreo
chewing. "That's all the candy you get," she informed
her pony, then turned to her partner. "That's just it, Beck,"
she continued as she slipped her foot in the stirrup and
pulled herself into the saddle. "People are careful about
what they say and do around the police, but when there's
just a couple of kids around, they don't worry about it
so much."

Becky nudged Oreo into a trot to catch up to
Ginger. "Maybe I don't want to hear everything people
say," she informed her friend. "We might find out something that will get us into a lot of trouble."

CHAPTER 8

The Alarm

As the girls reached the lane leading to Shamrock Stables, they reined their ponies to a halt. On the left was a sign shaped like a three-leaf clover with the words "Shamrock Stables" written in green lettering against a white background.

"Hm," said Becky, leaning to the side of her saddle to get a better look, "that makes sense."

"What makes sense?"

"Why Freddie's barn colors are green and white," answered Becky, pointing to the sign.

"The shamrock is a three-leaf clover," Amy Jo explained. "It's the national emblem of Ireland, and Freddie's grandmother was Irish."

Becky studied the sign again. "I didn't know it was the national emblem of Ireland," she said. "But, then you're half Irish, so you'd know stuff like that."

Lifting herself from the saddle, Amy Jo stood up in her stirrups and craned her neck toward the paddock at Crooked Oak Farm. "No sign of Midnight Magic," she said, easing herself back down again.

Becky stretched up in her saddle as well straining to see the stallion. "Mr. Rumble must be keeping him in his stall."

"Maybe he's worried about Midnight Magic getting stolen, too," she reflected as the girls moved down the lane to the barn.

"Don't even think about it," replied Becky.

At the sound of hooves hitting the gravel, Toby came bounding out of the barn with Freddie ambling behind. The yellow Lab swallowed his barks and began to whimper as the girls reined in their ponies in front of the stable.

"Hi, Freddie," said both girls softly.

Freddie reached up to hold both ponies' reins as the girls hopped down, then lifted his hat a few inches off his head. "Mornin', girls," he greeted. But the smile from before was missing.

Amy Jo drew the reins over Ginger's head. "I was sorry to hear about Flash, Freddie," she said, working the buckle on her reins between her fingers.

Becky stepped forward. "We don't want to be in the way," she said, biting her lip nervously, "but we'll be glad to help you if you need us," she finished, then glanced at Amy Jo who nodded and smiled.

Freddie looked at the ground, blinking back sudden tears. "It's about as bad as it can get, girls. My dreams have all turned to a nightmare now that Flash has gone missing." He shook his head and reached down to comfort his dog. "Toby hasn't been the same either. Been layin' in Flash's stall all day, his head resting on his paws. Have to carry his food into the stall, but he hardly touches it. Have to drag him into the house at night." Freddie placed his hands on his knees as he leaned down to speak to his dog. "Gotta eat, Toby. Can't lose you, too."

Amy Jo glanced at Becky who was blinking back tears as well. "Uh," she began, then swallowed hard and

ran the back of her hand across her eyes.
"We didn't know if you'd heard about
Tommy."

Freddie looked up, and she continued. "He's been
arrested," she said softly.

Freddie's ashened face registered shock. "Tommy?
Been arrested you say."

When the girls nodded their heads, Freddie stumbled
over to a bench near the barn door and sat down hard. "They
think Tommy had something to do with Flash being
stolen?" he murmured to himself. "He's kind of a rough-
talkin' fellow, but why would Tommy do a thing like that?"

Freddie's eyes focused on the ground; his breath
came in shallow spurts. Freddie pulled himself up straight
and looked at the girls. "I can't believe Tommy would do
this." He eased himself up from the bench and began
pacing back and forth working a piece of straw between his
teeth as he walked. "He hoped Flash would win the race,
he did, no matter what the police think," he muttered.
Suddenly he stopped and turned to the girls. "Where's
Tommy now? They haven't put him in jail have they?"

Becky pushed her hair behind her ear and cleared
her throat. "Well, actually, Officer Higgins arrested
Tommy and locked him up just before we rode out here."

Freddie shook his head as he sat down on the
bench again. "Officer Higgins was out here yesterday
investigatin', askin' a bunch of questions. But I never thought
he suspected one of my own people." He sighed deeply, then
looked up. "Arrested Tommy just *now*, you say?"

Amy Jo nodded. "Just before we came out."

Freddie's eyes widened. "Did he say why he was
arrestin' Tommy . . . what the evidence was?"

Becky looked from Amy Jo to Freddie. "No, Amy Jo asked him a bunch of questions, but he said everything would be in the paper tomorrow."

Amy Jo looked down at the older man. "Did the police find anything when they were out here yesterday?"

Freddie rubbed the back of his neck. "They searched through all the lockers and tack trunks," he began. "Dumped out the trash cans and sorted through all that stuff. Tried to take fingerprints off Flash's stall, but said they were all too smudged."

"Hm," said Amy Jo as Toby walked over and licked her hand. "Did Toby bark during the night when Flash was stolen?"

Freddie shook his head. "I didn't hear a peep out of him."

Amy Jo gave Becky a look that said, *I wonder why Toby didn't bark*, then looked thoughtfully down to the end of the lane. "How do you suppose someone drove a horse van in here, took Flash out of his stall, loaded him up, then drove back down the lane without anyone hearing the motor running on the truck?" she asked, a frown creasing her forehead as she looked quizzically at Freddie.

Freddie raised his eyebrows. "Couldn't happen that way," he answered, taking the straw from his mouth as he stood up and pointed down the lane. "There's a sensor right there as you pass the shamrock sign at the beginning of the lane, and it beeps in the house if anybody crosses it, day or night."

Becky lowered her head, then lifted it again as an idea struck her. "You mean a horse van couldn't have passed through the front gate in the middle of the night because the sensor would have beeped in your house?"

"That's about it," Freddie replied.  "Except when Ned pulled in around 6:00 a.m. for work, that sensor didn't go off from the time I went to bed last night until Rubble pulled his van down the lane at 6:30 a.m. yesterday morning," he continued. "As soon as I heard the sensor go off, I quickly grabbed Charlie out of bed, threw some clothes on him, and we headed down here. Charlie wanted to see that race in the worst way. Made me promise to get him up to watch it."

Becky piped up. "So, that means somebody must have led him off cross country somewhere. We could look for hoof prints."

"That's a good idea, Beck," Amy Jo began, "but horses ride around here all the time. Even if somebody did take him cross country, you'd never be able to pick up Flash's hoof prints in a million years."

Becky thought about that for a second and realized that her friend was correct.

Freddy nodded his agreement. "Police figured that, too," said Freddie, then pressed his lips together before he continued. "There's a reason why Flash couldn't have been led out of his stall that night."

Amy Jo looked up quickly. "Why's that?"

Freddie screwed his eyes up. "There's an alarm rigged to Flash's stall. The switch that turns it on and off is in the kitchen," he said, stabbing his index finger in the direction of the house for emphasis. "If somebody unlatches the stall while the alarm is set, it rings next to my bed. I always switch it on after all the men leave the barn at night, and don't turn it off until Ned pulls down the lane the next morning at six o'clock."

CHAPTER 9

Suspect Everybody

Amy Jo wiped the sweat from her forehead with the sleeve of her shirt. "These racehorses take up entirely too much space," she complained, peering into a stall. "Would you look at the size of this thing? I mean you could store two or three elephants in here, no problem. It seems like the stalls doubled in size."

Overnight the temperature had shot up ten degrees, and everyone's temper had gone right up with it.

Becky swept the last trace of straw from the aisle. "Freddie's barn is sure a lot bigger than mine," she sighed as she hung her broom next to the two others along the wall. "But at least we're done mucking out stalls and sweeping the aisle for the day."

"Yeah," Amy Jo said without much enthusiasm. "Six more days until Huey returns from vacation."

Becky gave her a look that said, *we need this job to pay for the ponies' expenses.*

"I know, I know. We need the money. I'm just tired," she admitted.

Becky collapsed on a stool next to the wash pit and closed her eyes.

Amy Jo walked to the middle of the aisle with a scrunchy in her mouth as she pulled her hair back into a ponytail. "Makes you wonder doesn't it?" she said out of the corner of her mouth.

Becky opened one eye. "Makes you wonder about what?"

Amy Jo doubled the scrunchy over her ponytail as she studied her friend. "Well, Tommy's out of the way now, so Ned can be exercise jockey again."

Becky blinked a couple of times. "What's that suppose to mean?" she asked. "Are you suspicious of Ned or something?"

"No more suspicious of him than anybody else," Amy Jo turned to leave with Becky scrambling off the stool to catch up. "I mean look at Mr. Rubble," she said in a low voice over her shoulder. "He stands to gain as much as anybody if Flash doesn't race against one of his racehorses at the track next week."

Becky glanced behind them and then whispered. "Whenever we're on a case, you always suspect everybody. All I'm saying is that Ned and Mr. Rubble are nice people."

Amy Jo reached the paddock first, then grabbed her bridle, and headed toward Ginger. "Nice people can be desperate and do bad things," she reminded her friend. "I mean look at Freddie. He hid the stopwatch right after he clocked Flash. Nobody knows how fast his horse ran on that track. Maybe Flash isn't as fast as Freddie's leading everybody to believe. Maybe he knows Flash *can't* win the race next week and he took him away in the middle of the night and hid him somewhere. I mean Freddie's the only one who can turn off those alarms in the middle of the night, you know."

Becky stared at Amy Jo. "But Freddie won't get any money if he hides his horse and pretends that he's stolen."

Amy Jo returned her friend's stare. "Did you ever think that Freddie might have Flash insured and that he might be able to collect insurance money if he's stolen?"

Becky felt sick. Somebody she knew and liked probably had something to do with Flash O' Lightning's disappearance. It was numbing.

Amy Jo studied her friend for a moment and decided that it was better to back off a little bit from her theories. "Oh, well, you're right," she said quickly. "Officer Higgins has got the right man. Anybody who's as big a creep as Tommy has got to be guilty."

It was time to tack up and go home. Ginger and Oreo enjoyed grazing in the large paddock at Shamrock Stables. Neither pony liked being caught when it was time to leave. As the girls walked towards the mares in the paddock, Ginger and Oreo walked just fast enough to maintain a frustrating two-step lead ahead of the girls.

Amy Jo pressed her lips together and squinted her eyes as she increased her pace. "I hope this isn't your idea of a good time, Ginger, because if you don't stop right now, I'm tossing out that bin full of carrots in Monday night's trash!"

Ginger flicked her ears back and forth a few times, exchanged a quick look with Oreo, then came to a dead stop.

Becky raised her eyebrows and looked at her friend. "Not bad!" she said, full of admiration. "We'll have to remember that threat the next time they pull this little stunt on us."

As the girls reached the edge of Crooked Oak Farm, Amy Jo pulled back gently on the reins.

Becky eyed her friend curiously. "Why'd you stop?"

Amy Jo chewed on her lower lip. "What do you say we pay a little visit to Mr. Rubble?" she asked, cocking her head to the side in a way that always made Becky jittery.

"Why?" asked Becky nervously. "We just saw him on Monday."

Amy Jo pulled on Ginger's left rein and nudged the pony down the hill with her heel. "Yeah, I know," she answered, "but I want to see if he has another black horse in his barn besides Midnight Magic."

Becky looked heavenward as if only a miracle could save her from what was sure to be a disastrous situation. "Maybe he's not home," she suggested hopefully.

Amy Jo's eyes lit up. "All the better," she said.

Ginger's reins were pulled over her head and tied to a fence under an oak tree. The pony turned her head around with mournful brown eyes itching to go home.

Becky passed her friend's mare and gave the pony a pat on the shoulder that said, *I know exactly how you feel*. "What are you going to do?" she asked Amy Jo as she fell into step.

Amy Jo rotated her neck in every direction for signs of activity. "Let's check all around the barn first to see if Mr. Rubble is here. If we can't find him outside, then we'll have to look for him in the barn," she said, her eyes twinkling at the mention of checking  out the barn.

Becky's shoulders sagged, and she nearly came to a stop. "Sounds like snooping to me, and I don't like the idea of getting caught one bit."

"Not snooping," Amy Jo corrected as she grabbed her friend by the arm, and dragged her along. "We're investigating. Come on, we only have a little ways to go and if we can't find him then we'll double back to the rear door," she explained. "Can't get caught if he's not around."

On the last lap, they crouched behind the truck and horse van for a moment and listened for any sounds of activity.

"Why, oh why, do we have to cross Crooked Oak Farm on the way home," Becky wailed softly to herself as she huddled behind her friend. "I should have guessed we'd end up like this . . . trespassing on private property. There's probably a hidden camera taking a picture of us right this very minute." Becky's eyes scanned along the roof line looking for a hidden camera. "And the pictures will be on Officer Higgins' desk first thing in the morning." She raised her voice slightly as Amy Jo resumed walking again. "We'll be handcuffed and locked up next to Tommy, you know. I can see the front page of the *Bedford Daily News*:

Two Girls Arrested
For Trespassing on Private Property

My Mom and Dad will come to see me every Thursday on visitation day." She began to sniff a little.

"Maybe bring me my favorite snack . . . chocolate chip cookies."

As they reached the back door, Amy Jo turned around. "Will you stop that blubbering and get a grip!" said Amy Jo impatiently.

Becky placed her hand on the door and looked directly at her friend. "Just what do you intend to say to him if he's in there?"

Amy Jo brushed her friend's hand away. "He's probably not in there," she said as she opened the door. "Anyway, if he is, I'll think of something."

The interior of the barn was dim and cool compared to the brillance and heat of the summer sun. Two steps inside, the girls stopped to get their bearings and allow their eyes time to adjust.

To the right was a door marked "Office" and to the left was the tack room where saddles and bridles hung in an orderly row.

Amy Jo stepped next to the closed office door, held her breath, and listened. She glanced at Becky, nodded her head, and gave her the thumbs-up. Quietly, they made their way to the main aisle.

As they rounded the corner, Midnight Magic's stall was the first one on the left. He stared at them and flicked his ears back and forth.

"Magic's still here," whispered Becky, looking through the metal bars. "Can we leave now?"

The stalls were different from Shamrock Stables. The upper part had metal bars for ventilation same as Freddie's barn, but the lower part was a solid piece of wood. The girls stood on their tiptoes to look over the bottom part to get a better look at Magic, but all they could see was his dark head.

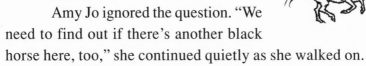

Amy Jo ignored the question. "We need to find out if there's another black horse here, too," she continued quietly as she walked on.

"There's Flint," whispered Becky as they walked past the next stall.

"Couldn't miss that gray gelding anywhere," agreed Amy Jo.

"Doesn't he have a chestnut mare, too?" asked Becky.

Amy Jo heard a horse stirring inside a stall and slipped across the aisle. "Yeah, here she is."

"That's it, then," said Becky relieved to be at the end of the aisle.

"Are you girls looking for something?" came a cold, deep voice from behind.

The girls spun around and there stood Mr. Rubble, hands on hips, his mouth drawn into a thin, straight line. Slowly, he moved towards them, his hands drawn into fists. An angry scowl deepened on his face.

"Do you want something, or are you just snooping around?" he asked.

CHAPTER 10

An Inside Job

Becky looked at Amy Jo with an *I told you so look in her eyes.*

"Well, uh," Amy Jo began, then cleared her throat, "actually, Beck wants to tell you something," she said, then turned expectantly to Becky whose mouth and eyes both popped open at the same time.

Mr. Rubble folded his arms and focused his attention on Becky; his patience grew thinner by the minute.

Becky looked over at the metal bars on Magic's stall and closed her eyes. "Metal bars," she muttered to herself, "that's where we'll be this time tomorrow."

Mr. Rubble frowned. "Speak up, girl," he said firmly. "I can't hear you." His hand strayed to his shirt pocket, but today it was empty.

"Metal bars," said Amy Jo quickly. "She's trying to tell you that Tommy's been arrested and he's behind bars at the Bedford jail."

Mr. Rubble's eyes narrowed. "I knew that. I just got back from town. The whole town knows that by now," he said in a voice that told them they had about two seconds to get down to business or get out. "Anything else?" he asked gruffly.

Amy Jo scratched her head for the two seconds he had allowed. "I don't think Becky has anything else she wants to say, right Beck?" she asked, raising her eyebrows to her friend.

Becky glared back, but made no response.

Amy Jo turned back to Mr. Rubble. "No, that's just about it," she continued, then took a deep breath and grabbed Becky by the arm. "Well, got to go, we'll be seeing you around."

They cut a wide path around Mr. Rubble and made a beeline for the rear door. Outside, the girls broke into a trot for the top of the hill and their ponies.

Once in the saddle and heading home Amy Jo cast a furtive glance at Becky. "Close call, huh, Beck?" she began, giving her friend another quick look. "Boy, I sure got us out of that one, didn't I?"

No answer.

They rode in silence for as long as Amy Jo could stand it, and then she said. "I guess you didn't think too much of it, did you?"

Slowly, Becky turned two fiery, hazel eyes at her riding buddy. "This whole thing was a waste of time," she began, almost too calmly. "There were only three horses in that barn and none of them were Flash O' Lightning."

Amy Jo knew she'd pushed her friend over the edge and did some fast, slick thinking. "Whew, look at the time! Way past lunch!" she said, throwing her arm with the watch on it in front of Becky. "Being hungry would put anyone in a bad mood," she raced on. "How about if we ride into Bedford, and I'll buy you a cheeseburger and some French fries at Ruthie's Cafe?" she suggested hopefully. Then added, "I'll throw in a milkshake, too. Chocolate be okay with you?"

Becky's eyes were slits, imbedded in a dull red face. "I told you I didn't want to go in there in the first place."

Amy Jo thought for a moment. "Okay, it was a dumb idea and a crummy thing to do to you and . . . I'm . . . I'm sorry. I really, really am sorry. I know a measly cheeseburger and French fries can't take back what I did, but at least I'm trying to make it up to you."

In the three months since Becky had moved to Bedford, she had never heard Amy Jo apologize like this. Slowly the anger slipped away and she turned to her friend. "Okay," she finally said. "I'm kind of hungry anyway."

Amy Jo relaxed her shoulders. "Good, because there's bound to be some people in there talking about Flash getting stolen, and I want to hear what everyone's saying," she added, then pressed her heels into Ginger's sides and cantered on ahead.

Becky shook her head as she watched her departing friend. "I should have known there was more to it than just trying to make it up to me."

*   *   *   *

After turning the ponies out in the paddock behind the ice cream store, they made their way down the alley and slipped into Ruthie's Cafe.

The girls stared. The cafe had booths next to the windows facing the outside on three sides, a few tables in the middle of the floor, and a counter with stools in the front.

"*Empty?*" Amy Jo wailed as she looked around the room. "What's the deal? It's only 2:00 p.m.; how come nobody's here?"

Becky walked over to the second booth on the right and slid into the seat. She propped her head up with her fist and closed her eyes. "I'm glad nobody's here," she began. "I'm tired and hungry, and all I want is to get something to eat and find a little corner to take a nap."

Amy Jo slipped into the booth across from her. "Some detective you are," she said, resting her elbows on the table. "We've got a case going and all you're thinking about is taking a nap."

Becky slowly opened her eyes and looked across the table at her friend. "That's not true," she said. "I'm also thinking of my stomach."

Amy Jo chuckled softly. "Yeah, I'm hungry too," she said.

Miss Ruthie walked up and pulled a pencil from behind her ear as she drew an order pad out of her apron pocket. "Hi, girls," she said. "What can I get you?"

"Two cheeseburgers with everything, French fries, and two chocolate shakes, please," said Amy Jo.

Becky straightened her shoulders and folded her hands. "I can order for myself," she explained to her partner.

"I thought that's what you wanted."

"I never said that's what I wanted," retorted Becky.

Miss Ruthie cast a surprised glance at the two friends who usually got along. "Would you like something different?"

"Yes," said Becky, clearing her throat. "I'd like a cheeseburger with everything, French fries, and a *strawberry* milkshake."

Miss Ruthie's eyes twinkled as she bit her lip. "Right, girls, it'll be ready in a jiffy," she said, then tore off the order and placed it on the shelf for the cook.

The girls were half finished with their lunch when two deputies from Lewisburg passed their window.

Amy Jo raised her eyebrows and rubbed her hands together. "Maybe they're coming in here. Things are looking up."

"If we're quiet, maybe they won't see us and we'll be able to hear what they say," suggested Becky.

Amy Jo's eyes widened. "Good thinking, Beck!" said Amy Jo in surprise. "Now you're acting like a real detective."

Becky stopped chewing. "I can't believe I actually said that."

"Me either," said Amy Jo, "but keep it coming."

The door to the cafe opened, and the girls slouched down in their seats as the deputies walked to the first booth directly behind them and sat down.

Miss Ruthie came from behind the counter and approached their booth, pencil and pad in hand. "Hello, deputies," she began. "What can I get for you?"

"A cheeseburger with everything, French fries, and a chocolate shake," said one of the deputies.

Amy Jo wagged her head from side to side and smiled devilishly.

"Make mine the same, except give me a strawberry shake instead," said voice number two.

Becky lifted her chin and eyebrows and rocked her head back and forth in time to her partner's motions.

"It's like this," came a man's hushed voice after Miss Ruthie had taken their order and left. "This deal about the note really bothers me."

Amy Jo sat stock still and shifted her weight. *A note?* This was something new. She turned her head and leaned forward across the table.

"What do you mean?" came the soft reply.

"Well, I just don't see how they can convict a man with that kind of note as part of the evidence."

Becky chewed quietly and leaned back against the seat.

"They found the note in his locker. I don't see what the problem is."

Amy Jo silently stole another French fry from her plate and slipped it into her mouth.

"Look, part of the note's been torn off," the first voice continued just above a whisper. "I mean the letters m-m-y are the only letters left of the person the note's addressed to. It might not be addressed to Tommy at all. It could be Sammy or Timmy or anybody whose name ends with m-m-y. Actually, we don't even know if it is somebody's name. The note could have been torn part way from the top and that's just another word in a sentence."

"Yes, but the point is that it was probably an inside job, and Tommy is the only person working on the inside who doesn't have an ironclad alibi. He said he was home watching TV all night, but nobody saw him. Now, take Ned. He was with Deputy Howard Allen and a bunch of guys watching football reruns until 2:00 in the morning. Then he  stayed overnight at one of the other guy's house."

"Yeah, yeah, I heard all about it," said the other deputy. "He was there until he went to work at 6:00 the next morning. No doubt about it. He was nowhere near the barn all night."

"Here you go, fellows," said Miss Ruthie as she placed their order in front of them.

Several minutes passed by while the men ate in silence.

"Okay, okay, I know what you're saying," said the first voice, still at a whisper. "But, what kind of fool would leave a hundred dollar bill in his locker as evidence that he was being paid to steal a horse? . . . Figure that one out if you can."

"So, he overlooked it, or it slipped out of his hand or something."

"But, where's the rest of the money? We can't find it anywhere."

"He hid it real well, that's all."

"Or maybe he never got it in the first place."

"Did you ever think that the rest of the money might still be at Shamrock Stables, but we haven't found it yet?"

Amy Jo and Becky exchanged wide-eyed glances while Amy Jo nodded her head and Becky shook hers.

"Officer Higgins thinks he'll come clean and confess where the rest of the money is," said the first deputy. "But if he didn't do it, he's not going to have much to confess."

"He did it all right. He just got sloppy."

"Well, he'll be sent to the county prison just as soon as they call and say they've got room for him. Then it'll be their problem. Meanwhile, they've got dozens of officers and horse lovers looking for that horse in every nook and cranny in every direction. It's like he disappeared into thin air. Like he's the phantom stallion or something."

"I've got news for you. There's no such thing as a ghost horse. He's somewhere, and we'll find him sooner or later."

Shuffling could be heard as the two men got up to leave. After they paid their bill and opened the door, the girls slouched down in their seats as the men passed the window on the way back to the police station.

"Hm," said Amy Jo sitting up in her booth.

Becky eyed her friend suspiciously. "What's that supposed to mean?"

"That means tonight we go back to Shamrock Stables and do some more looking around."

"Well, we can't ride up the lane or it'll set off the sensor," said Becky, knitting her eyebrows.

Amy Jo sat up in surprise. "Good thinking again, Beck. I almost forgot."

Becky shook her head. "I don't know what's getting into me," she said, staring at her friend. "Anyway, what's the deal? We're going to be there tomorrow morning for work. We can look around then."

"Yeah, but people will be watching us then," Amy Jo leaned over the table. "Okay, here's what we'll do. I'll ride my bike back to your place about 8:00 tonight," she began, "by then they'll have the horses at Shamrock Stables settled for the night and the barn should be empty."

Becky closed her eyes. "This is the part I hate," she admitted. "Checking out places after dark."

Amy Jo lifted her palms up. "The place will be empty," she said. "There aren't going to be any problems."

Becky covered her face with her hands. "Where have I heard that before?"

CHAPTER 11

Go Find Him, Boy!

There was a short cut from the Allison Farm to Shamrock Stables. The girls would have used it on their way to work, but that would have taken them past the practice ring. Tommy always got irritated if the horse he was riding was distracted by the girls walking by on their ponies. So, every morning they trotted down the line of oak trees on Mr. Rubble's property to Quarry Road. They rode along Quarry Road for a short distance, then turned up Freddie's driveway to the barn. It took longer, but then Tommy didn't grumble at them.

But, that night they took the shortcut. They tied up the ponies on the back end of the practice track behind the blind spot. The blind spot hid everything from the house, so that even if Freddie happened to be looking out a window, he wouldn't see the girls or the mares. There was a half moon shining in the night sky. All the more reason to be careful.

The girls sneaked into the barn through the rear door and drew out their tiny flashlights from the pockets of their jeans.

Becky swallowed hard as her eyes scanned the barn. Everything appeared so different at night. The openings to the stalls were like black holes. It didn't take much imagination to picture someone lurking in the shadows. At that moment she regretted asking Miss Ruthie for a refill on her strawberry milkshake. "What should we look for?" she asked, trying to hold her flashlight steady.

"Anything that looks suspicious," said Amy Jo predictably. She stepped up to Flash's stall and shined the light on the walls. She got down flat on the ground and scooted like a lizard underneath the door. Didn't dare touch the door itself for fear of setting off the alarm in the house.

"Well, what exactly does that mean?" asked Becky.

"Uh, money hidden or the other part of the note or something that looks out of place. You know," she said turning to face Becky, "stuff like that."

Becky looked puzzled. She found it difficult to believe that two sixth graders would be able to discover something that trained police officers had failed to find. "Don't you think that Officer Higgins and his men would have found those kinds of things?"

"Look," Amy Jo explained trying to be patient, "anybody can overlook something. Freddie is going to lose the farm if he doesn't get Flash back. So, don't you think that this is the least we can do for him?"

Amy Jo would have to bring that up. Becky nodded her head and slowly felt her way down to the lockers where the men kept their gear. Soon, she was on her hands and knees looking under and behind everything.

"Hm, that's odd," mumbled Amy Jo.

Becky returned to Flash's stall and watched intently as Amy Jo focused her light on the wall in front of her. "What's odd?"

Amy Jo turned around. "Scooch  under the door . . . be careful not to touch it. I want to show you something."

Becky carefully wiggled under the door and came to stand where her partner was waiting. "What have you got?"

Amy Jo shone the light on a spot that was about their eye level. "It's probably nothing, but we've cleaned this stall about eight times and I don't ever remember seeing this spot."

Becky leaned forward and squinted into the center of the round light. "It just looks like a little white powder that's all," she commented.

"Yeah, I know it looks like a little white powder . . . almost like baby powder," said Amy Jo. "But, the wood in here is dark. I think I'd remember seeing a dab of white powder on the wall."

Becky took a sniff of the powder from about an inch away. "Smells a little like baby powder," she decided.

The clanging of the latch on the stall door shattered the silence. The light over their heads glared as it was switched on.

"What are you looking for?"

It was Charlie. And he had Toby with him.

The girls slumped against the wall and closed their eyes. Amy Jo held her hand to her chest. Becky's hand flew to her stomach.

"I can hardly breath," said Amy Jo between gasps.

Becky's other hand hovered around her mouth. "I think I'm going to throw up," she said in a muffled voice.

"What's the matter?" asked Charlie stepping closer to the girls. "I didn't scare you did I?"

"No, no, no," said Amy Jo, sliding down the wall to the floor. "Just take me to the hospital," she continued, hand still clutching her chest. "Tell your grandfather thanks for giving us this job and everything."

Becky pushed herself away from the wall. She patted Charlie reassuringly on the shoulder with one hand while keeping the other one securely on her midsection. "It's alright, Charlie," she whispered, not trusting her voice.

Suddenly, Amy Jo bolted upright. "Charlie! You opened the stall door!"

Charlie turned around and looked at the opening. "Yep," he agreed.

"The alarm will go off!" Becky had figured it out, too.

Charlie shook his head. "No, Grandpa hasn't turned on the alarm to the stall since Flash was stolen," he said confidently.

In their relief, both girls forgot their aches and pains.

Charlie looked for a clean piece of straw to put between his lips. "Whatcha doing out here anyway?" he asked. "Did you lose something?"

Amy Jo flipped off her flashlight and placed it back in her pocket. "No, we're just trying to help Officer Higgins," she explained, somewhat vaguely.

Becky led the way out of the stall, then turned and closed Flash's door. "I guess we'd better call it quits and go home," she suggested.

"How did you get here?" asked Charlie.

"We crossed over Mr. Rubble's  property," explained Amy Jo. "Same as always."

"Where's Ginger and Oreo?" pressed Charlie. "Or did you walk?"

Becky headed towards the back door. "They're out back," she began. "We have them tied to the practice ring fence."

"I'll walk with you," said Charlie, trailing along with Toby not far behind.

A thought suddenly occurred to Amy Jo, and she turned her head around to look at Charlie. "What brought you out to the barn this time of night?" she asked.

Charlie took three quick steps and caught up to the girls. "Grandpa fell asleep on the couch in front of the TV set. Then, Toby started whining at the door and Grandpa didn't hear him. So, I thought I'd just take him outside," he said. "Then Toby ran to the barn and I had to follow him. I guess he must have heard you."

Amy Jo looked over at Becky. "Good thing Toby knows us or he'd be barking all over the place."

In silence they walked to the other end of the track. Ginger and Oreo lifted their heads and neighed softly as they heard everyone approach.

Just as the girls untied their ponies Toby placed his sniffing nose to the ground and began to whimper. The whimper grew to a growl which progressed to a bark. The girls desperately tried to stop the noise lest it wake Freddie.

"Charlie!" yelled Becky frantically. "Make him stop!"

Charlie looked at the Lab then turned to the girls. "When this happens with Lassie on TV, they always say

89

'go find it, girl' or something like that. And then Lassie goes off sniffing the ground and everybody follows her."

Amy Jo turned to Charlie with a look of superiority that eleven year olds reserve for six year olds. "Look, Charlie," she began, placing her hand on her hip, "Toby is not Lassie, and he is not going to track down Flash O' Lightning by following his scent. Okay?"

Charlie's philosophy was, "It never hurts to try" so he kneeled down beside the Lab and said, "Go find him, boy!"

Amy Jo scoffed while Becky looked on sympathetically, but all three of them scrambled when Toby took off at a trot towards the woods.

"Quick!" Amy Jo threw her leg over Ginger's saddle then reached down for Charlie's arm. She settled the little boy behind her and turned her pony around to follow Toby. "Hold on, Charlie!" she said as he secured his arms around her waist.

Becky tightened the girth, mounted her pony, and took off at a canter until she'd caught up with the rest. "You can't really think he's leading us to Flash can you?" she asked.

"Sure!" Charlie replied.

"Who knows?" answered Amy Jo. "Baby powder on Flash's stall is the only clue we have so far. We may as well see where Toby leads us."

Becky looked doubtfully at the other two. "Well, I guess it doesn't hurt to follow along."

They tailed Toby into the woods, retracing their steps a half a dozen times. The woods hid the moon and was full of sounds that are only creepy after dark. The oak trees were giants with huge arms that  reached out to grab them as the limbs swayed in the growing breeze. An old tree stump was like a bear ready to pounce on them as they passed it. Charlie squeezed his eyes shut as the girls pressed their ponies as far to the right of the stump as the path would allow them.

Half a dozen times the girls were ready to turn back when Toby lead them to a clearing near a small, gravel back road. The moon was higher now and shone more brightly. The girls reined in their ponies and looked nervously about, then watched in fascination as the dog walked briskly in a circle sniffing frantically. He appeared to pick up the scent again, then hurried down to Quarry Road. They trotted past the entrance to Shamrock Stables and, for the second time that day, were headed towards Crooked Oak Farm.

"This is impossible. We were here earlier today . . . even searched the barn," said Becky. "Flash is just not here."

Amy Jo's gaze trailed along the edge of the barn looking for Mr. Rubble. Suddenly, her mind's eye remembered an object she'd seen earlier in the day, and her chin dropped to her chest. "I am so dumb," she said in disgust. "I cannot believe that I didn't put two and two together right away. I was so worried about getting into the barn that I missed the most obvious clue of all."

Becky looked at her partner in surprise. "What do you mean?" she asked.

"Come on, I'll show you," said Amy Jo, nudging her pony forward.

CHAPTER 12

A Hiding Place

They loosened the girths on the ponies and tied them behind a row of shrubs. There was enough slack so that Ginger and Oreo could nibble away on the grass. It was important to keep the mares quiet.

Charlie and the girls crouched down behind the shrubs. They parted some low limbs just enough to peek through at the darkened barn while Toby lay panting beside Ginger and Oreo. Everything was quiet, just like at Shamrock Stables.

"Charlie," began Amy Jo, "why don't you stay here with Toby and the ponies while Beck and I take another look at the barn."

Charlie's eyes doubled in size. "No, way," he said looking around at the eerie shadows. "I'm going with you."

Becky grabbed Amy Jo by the arm and swung her around. "Now look," she said. Her stomach had reached the end of its rope. "Unless you can come up with a really great reason for going in there again I am heading for home."

"Okay, Beck," said Amy Jo in a voice that was none too steady. She could see that her partner was ready to bolt and run. "Do you remember when Mr. Rubble told us that his horse van had a flat tire and that he'd have to borrow one to bring Midnight Magic down here?"

Becky thought about the conversation they'd had with Mr. Rubble the day he first told them about Midnight Magic. "Yeah, I remember. He said he could borrow one at the track."

"Well, when we stood behind the horse van today checking to see if anybody was around, did you notice anything odd about the van?" asked Amy Jo, eyeing Becky closely.

Becky blinked her eyes a couple of times. "Not really," she finally admitted.

Amy Jo leaned in closer to Becky. "None of the tires were flat," she explained. "Why would he need to borrow another van if his tires were okay?"

"He lied about it," said Becky softly.

Charlie had stepped between the girls and watched each girl intently as she spoke. "Why did he lie about it?" asked Charlie softly.

Both girls had nearly forgotten about him. Now, with mixed feelings, they looked down at the little boy. He wanted to go with them. But, maybe he was the type that wailed hysterically if things didn't go right. Perhaps they should take him home first.

Amy Jo looked at her watch. It was getting late. "Look, Charlie," she began, "I'm a little nervous about taking you in there with us. Are you the type that cries real loud when he gets scared?"

Charlie looked up with solemn eyes. "Not me," he said. "I cry real soft when I get scared. But I won't cry at all 'cause I'm taking Toby along and he'll take care of me."

Amy Jo looked down at the yellow Lab. The dog suddenly glowed like a neon light. This was like a bad movie. It was utterly hopeless. The dog would bark and Charlie would sob hysterically ... unbelievable. "No choice, Beck," she finally decided. "We'll have to take both of them with us."

"Right," answered Becky, shrugging her shoulders. "No choice."

"Okay," Amy Jo sighed. "Charlie, you and Toby follow right behind me. Beck, you bring up the rear. Everybody got it?"

Becky and Charlie nodded. Toby seemed to understand that he was part of the team and fell into step beside Charlie.

Naturally, the barn door creaked as they opened it. Everyone scurried inside and flattened themselves against the wall. Toby still panted and Charlie alternately held his breath and gasped for air. A U-Haul could be rattling down the aisle and they'd never hear it. Nobody closed in around them so they edged on down the wall, slipped around the corner, and stopped at the first stall.

Moonlight pouring in from the windows was just bright enough that Amy Jo found a switch right next to Magic's stall. Carefully she turned it on, ready to flip it off quickly if the light shone on the entire barn rather than just inside the stallion's stall. Luck finally smiled on them as the light bulb flickered on in the horse's stall. Midnight Magic turned around and stepped to the front, hoping it was time for his grain. He tossed his head and pawed with his hoof.

Toby whimpered softly and jumped up on the door stretching his neck trying to see the horse.

Magic pressed his head against the bars and looked down. He blew air from his nostrils and nickered.

"Do you see what I see?" said Amy Jo grabbing a nearby stool.

Becky, petrified that Toby would bark, was too busy soothing him to notice anything else. "Right now I don't want to see anything except the back door on our way out."

"Me either," echoed Charlie shakily. "I think I have to use the bathroom. How long we gonna be here?"

Amy Jo ignored both of them as she slid the stool in front of the stall and stood on it. Magic still had his head plastered to the bars looking at Toby. "Well, I'll be . . . ," she whispered.

"You'll be what?" asked Charlie, for a second, more curious than afraid.

"What do you see?" asked Becky, anxiously stepping forward.

"Beck," commanded Amy Jo in a low voice. "Find a rag or something and dip it in one of the horse's water buckets. Hurry!"

Becky left the Lab's side and walked in circles for a moment until she found a rag. She raced back to Amy Jo's side after dampening it in a bucket.

Amy Jo slowly lifted the rag up to the horse's head murmuring soft, encouraging words, then gently rubbed in a corner of his head.

Becky forgot to be afraid as she watched intently. What did her partner think she was doing? Suddenly, some of the pieces fell into place as Amy Jo held out the rag for her to see. "It has a black spot on it," Becky exclaimed softly. "And there's a white, jagged mark where you've been rubbing."

"More like the shape of a lightning  bolt, wouldn't you say?" Amy Jo remarked.

Charlie looked up. "Lightning?" he asked. "Flash O' Lightning has a lightning shape on his forehead."

"Sure does," Amy Jo confirmed as she stepped down from the stool. "I think it's time to call Officer Higgins."

Charlie grabbed hold of Toby's collar. "Does that mean we're going to leave?" he asked hopefully.

"We're leaving," Becky said firmly.

Amy Jo shoved the stool back where she'd found it, threw the rag in the corner, and flipped off the light. "Charlie, we'll drop you and Toby off at your house, then Beck and I are heading down to the police station. Officer Higgins is going to hear about this."

The sound of a truck pulling behind the barn stopped them dead in their tracks.

Everyone, including Toby, looked at Amy Jo. "Quick," she whispered frantically. "Let's go to one of the empty stalls!"

They fumbled past the stall where Flash O' Lightning was being kept and turned into an empty one near the end. Earlier in the day they had been disgusted about the bottom half of the stalls being solid wood. Now, it became a hiding place. They crouched down with Toby between Becky and Charlie. Both stroked the dog's shoulders trying to keep him quiet.

Amy Jo sat on the end next to Charlie stroking his head trying to keep him from blubbering.

The rear door was opened and the barn light turned on. As long as no one came into their stall, and everyone stayed quiet, they were safe.

They heard the office door creek on its hinges and a telephone receiver being lifted off its cradle.

"Look, this is Rubble," said the voice. "We've got to move him out tonight." There was silence for a few seconds, then he added. "No, I lost it somewhere today. I'm calling from the office phone." More silence. "Because those two girls were snooping around here today that's why. I got a real bad feeling about those two. How soon can you get here?" A short pause and then. "Okay, I'll hook the horse van up to my truck. See you in five minutes."

The telephone clattered as it was thrown back into its cradle. There were retreating footsteps and the sound of the door closing, after that, dead silence.

Everyone sat still for the first full moment, then the pressure behind the dam broke and Charlie let out a wail followed by a series of sobs.

"Charlie, Charlie, get a grip," Amy Jo began desperately. "We only have to be quiet for a little while. They'll be back soon and if they don't hear us we'll be okay." Amy Jo looked in the direction of Becky. "I thought he said he cried softly."

Becky took a deep breath. "I'm ready to bawl myself," she said rather unsteadily. "It'll take Mr. Rubble a while to hook up the van and the other person isn't suppose to get here for a few minutes. Do you think we ought to make a run for it?"

"There's a chance we might get caught trying to get away. We've got to get a hold of Officer Higgins and let him know where we are." Amy Jo covered her head with her hands and thought. Within seconds she had a plan. "Let's try this . . . Charlie, you stay here with Toby for just a minute. Beck, you come with me and look out the door for Mr. Rubble while I use the  phone to call Officer Higgins. Okay?" Not waiting for an answer, she patted Charlie on the head, then took his arms and placed them securely around Toby. "You're doing fine, Charlie." He was still crying, but now they were silent tears.

Becky raced with her partner down the aisle and eased the door open while Amy Jo stepped into the office. She couldn't see Mr. Rubble, but she could hear him around the corner hooking up the van to the truck.

Amy Jo dialed the number from memory. She beat her knuckles on the desk while she waited for someone to answer. "Hello!" she said, after what seemed like ages. "No! I can't hold," she nearly shouted, but it was too late. "Beck, what's happening outside?"

Becky turned her head and leaned towards the office. "He's still working on the van."

Suddenly, the door was ripped from Becky's hand and she screamed. The entire barn was flooded with light.

It was Ned.

Amy Jo slowly lowered the phone and returned it to its cradle.

No one spoke for what seemed like an eternity, then Ned opened his mouth. "So, now you know. I wanted to just slip out of town with the horse without anybody ever finding out."

"I thought we had five minutes?" Amy Jo's voice sounded strangely hollow. "How'd you get here so fast?"

"Rubble called me on my cell phone," Ned explained. "I was in my truck a half mile away."

"What are you going to do to us?" asked Becky bravely.

Ned drew his brows together and leaned against the door. "I don't know yet. Rubble's not going to like this," he said, then stepped back and called softly. "Rubble, Rubble, in here, quick."

Seconds later Mr. Rubble came bursting through the door. He took one look at the girls and heaved a disgusted sigh. "This is what I was worried about!" he said, hitting the flat of his hand against the wall. "Only now we'll have to *deal* with them!"

The girls exchanged nervous glances. They didn't like the way he emphasized the word "deal."

Ned stared at the girls with mixed emotions. "Let's not be too hasty. Horse stealing is one thing, but we're going to have to deal with this situation carefully."

There it was again . . . that word "deal." And on top of that, they weren't even human beings. They were a "situation." It was a lot easier to "deal" with a "situation" than to think of them as real people.

Beads of sweat appeared on Mr. Rubble's upper lip. "What do you have in mind?" he asked.

Ned wiped his mouth with the back of his hand. "Look, let's load Flash into the van," he began. "I saw the girls' ponies as I came up the driveway. We can load them beside Flash."

"What about the girls?"

Ned looked at Amy Jo and then at Becky. "We can put them in the backseat of the truck. We'll drive to the state line and drop them off in the country. I know a place that's far enough from any house that it'll take hours for the girls to find someone."

Mr. Rubble took out his handkerchief and dabbed at his forehead. "I don't know if it will work, but

I don't have a better idea, so we may as well
start with yours."

Ned took Becky by the arm and
guided her into the office beside Amy Jo. "Where's your
key, Rubble?" he asked. "Rip out the phone cord so they
can't call for help, then lock them in here until we get
Flash and the ponies loaded on the van. We'll come back
for them after that."

CHAPTER 13

Clever Scheme

Becky turned to Amy Jo, her lips trembling. "Now we're in big trouble, and what are you going to do about it?" she demanded as a tear slid down her cheek.

Amy Jo yanked on all the desk drawers hoping she'd find one unlocked with a key to the office door in it. "What am I going to do?" she asked as her fingers moved along the bottom of the desk still looking for a hidden key.

Becky folded her arms and pulled them tightly to her body. "Yeah, what are you going to do?" she asked again, steadying her voice.

Amy Jo had finished her inspection of the desk and swivel chair and turned to face Becky. "I don't have a clue," she finally admitted.

"Well, you picked a fine time to run out of ideas!"

"Well, you know I wouldn't be just shattered if you came up with something on your own," Amy Jo suggested, licking her lips, then drying them with her hand.

"It wasn't my idea to come here in the first place!"

"I know, I know," said Amy Jo, still looking around the room trying to figure out what to do. "Look, let's be real quiet and listen through the door. Maybe we'll find something out."

"A lot of good that'll do us," objected Becky. "We're still locked up in here."

"At least we'll know what's going on," said Amy Jo as she pressed her ear to the door.

"What's that sound?" they heard Ned ask.

There was shuffling and then Mr. Rubble's reply. "Wonderful!" he said sarcastically. "I suppose you want to take the kid and the dog along, too. Just pile everybody in the truck!"

"No, the dog'll bark . . . maybe even bite," Ned decided. "Just shut the stall door. They can't unlatch it from the inside anyway. It'll be tomorrow before someone finds them."

The sound of Flash's hoofs clopping on the cement floor was nearly drowned out by Toby's barks and Charlie's sobs.

Finally, the door was unlocked. The girls backed up, one further than the other. Mr. Rubble was quicker and took Becky by the arm. Ned grunted and sighed as he manhandled Amy Jo out of the barn. Amy Jo's riding boots created miniature railroad tracks that could be seen the entire distance from the barn to the truck. Moments later the truck pulled the van down Quarry Road and headed out of town.

The back seat was cramped and the girls sat glued together. They would have sat glued together anyway, but this gave them an opportunity to whisper to each other without changing positions.

Becky placed her mouth near Amy Jo's ear. "What do you think?" she whispered.

"What do you mean what do I think?" asked Amy Jo, trying to maintain a brave front.

"Well . . . maybe we could talk them into letting us go if we promised not to tell anyone until tomorrow." It was dark in the back seat, but Becky didn't need the light to know the expression on her friend's face.

"Fat chance," Amy Jo whispered back. "Let's get them talking," she suggested. "Maybe they'll get sick of us and decide to let us go early."

"That doesn't sound like a very good idea," offered Becky in a panic. "They might get too sick of us and then who knows what they might do."

Amy Jo cleared her throat and leaned forward. "Where are we going?" she asked, trying to keep her voice steady.

Nobody said anything.

"Heading west maybe?"

More silence.

"East then?" suggested Amy Jo.

Ned was driving and looked over at Mr. Rubble, then turned his head to glance in the back before returning his attention to the road. "We'll let you go in a couple of hours. Just sit tight."

"Well, look, Ned," pressed Amy Jo again, "why are you doing this? Freddie didn't do anything to you."

Ned hesitated for a moment. "After my accident, I was in the hospital for three weeks and then in the rehabilitation hospital for a long time learning to walk all over again. I'm in debt up to my eyeballs!" he continued bitterly. "I could've paid it off if Freddie had given me my old job back as exercise rider. I don't want to be in debt the rest of my life."

The girls thought about that for a moment, then Becky found the courage to ask what had stumped them both. "How did you get Flash O' Lightning out of his stall without setting off the alarm?"

Mr. Rubble chuckled once, then broke into an ugly laughter that lasted for a full minute. "I never thanked you girls for helping me out." And he laughed again.

Becky cut loose. "We would never help you steal Freddie's horse!" she began heatedly while Amy Jo poked her in the side. "How could you say something like that?"

Mr. Rubble only laughed louder.

Now Becky was really ticked. "You're lying!"

Mr. Rubble stopped laughing. "Oh, you think I'm lying do you, little girl?" he said with a hard edge to his voice. "Okay, well you just listen to this. After Freddie bought Flash O' Lightning, all I could think about was getting that horse for myself. Ned's not the only one who's in debt up to his eyeballs. I lost all my racehorses . . . everything. I knew that if I could get my hands on Flash O' Lightning I could start up again. I could take him far away in another state where nobody had ever seen the horse and then I'd be okay."

Mr. Rubble hesitated for a few seconds before continuing. "And then it happened. I was at a stable about thirty miles away and saw a horse that was Flash's double except he didn't have a lightning flash down his forehead. The idea hit me like a ton of bricks . . . switch horses."

Amy Jo waited for him to continue. When he didn't, she asked. "How'd you switch them?"

Mr. Rubble settled into his seat. He seemed to enjoy recounting his clever scheme. "The problem was

how to get Magic into Flash's stall for only
a short time so that no one would get a
real good look at him. I mean Magic looks
a whole lot like Flash, but he wouldn't fool anybody for
more than a minute up close . . . especially on the racetrack. Then, I met you girls on the hill that day when you
were leaving Shamrock Stables after work. You said . . . ,"
And he started laughing again.

The upside to this conversation was that Amy Jo
forgot she was terrified and began to get angry. "We didn't
say anything about stealing Freddie's horse!" she said
hotly.

"We'd never hurt Freddie!" chimed in Becky.

Mr. Rubble gulped down his laughter and continued. "You said 'how about if Flash O' Lightning and
Midnight Magic race?'" He turned in his seat and smirked
at them. "And that's when everything came together.
I called Ned on my cell phone, and we talked about it.
We had to make the switch before Flash could be
identified by a tattoo. So, we set the race for Wednesday
morning. Tuesday after Tommy's practice session seemed
to be the best time to make the switch. There's a blind
spot on the back of the track, you know."

"Yeah," said Amy Jo, "we know where it is."

"I told Ned I'd meet him there," he continued as
if he were reliving a great moment in his life. "I had
parked the horse van in a side road on the other side of
the woods, and walked Magic to the back side of the track
where nobody could see us. I slid a row of poles out of
their holes to make an opening in the fence, and when
Ned came around the bend, we switched horses. Ned put
Flash's cooling blanket on Magic and that covered up his

whole body and most of his legs. I took Flash, put the poles back in their holes and led him through the woods and out to that little back road. When I drove down Quarry Road anybody who saw me thought I had picked up Midnight Magic at the racetrack and was taking him to my barn."

The girls sat dumbfounded. Finally Amy Jo asked, "How'd you get the mark on his forehead?"

Mr. Rubble rubbed his chin. "Oh, that," he said. "Well, Ned traced the mark on Flash's forehead with a piece of paper and cut it out, then I fed Magic a couple of carrots to distract him while Ned placed the paper over the horse's forehead. Ned sprayed the outline with hair spray to make it sticky and then coated it with baby powder. All I had to do was put some dirt on Flash's forehead to hide his mark."

Becky thought of another problem. "But, didn't you think you'd get caught Wednesday morning taking Magic out of Flash's stall?"

Ned jumped in. "It sure worried *me!*" he admitted. "I got there earlier than usual, got a rag and wiped what was left of the baby powder off Magic's forehead. I had Rubble's saddle and bridle that I'd snuck into the barn from my car. Quick as I could, I put them on Magic and took him out when I heard the van pull in front of the barn. Rubble had backed up to the door close enough that Freddie couldn't see the back of the van or the barn door from the house. When he came around the corner, we pretended that Magic had just been unloaded and I got all excited because Flash wasn't in his stall."

There was another pause while the girls digested what had been said.

Another thought occurred to Amy Jo and she turned to Mr. Rubble. "But, you'd end up with two horses at Crooked Oak. What if somebody came looking and saw both of them there at the same time?"

"Nope," said Mr. Rubble arrogantly. "When I left Shamrock Stables that Wednesday morning, I told Freddie I was taking Magic back to the barn and then returning the trailer to the track. What nobody realized was that I drove over to my barn, hid it around the corner for a few minutes, then turned around and drove back down the driveway again. When I returned the trailer, Magic was inside. I was really taking him back where I'd gotten him. Told the man there I'd changed my mind and didn't want to buy him after all. So, the only black horse in the stall was Flash O' Lightning, but everyone thought it was Midnight Magic."

They'd thought of everything. "We planned to keep Flash at the barn for a few days, then tell my landlord I was leaving town. My lease was up in another few weeks anyway, the other horses in the barn belonged to my landlord, so whose business was it if I decided to leave town a little ahead of schedule. Nobody would have thought anything of it."

Ned ran his hand through his hair. "Yeah, but I wasn't supposed to join you for another month," he worried. "By that time, the trial would be over and Tommy would have been found guilty. And now this," he continued, jerking his thumb towards the back seat.

Silence settled in for a while. The girls looked outside, but they were in the country and it was too dark to see anything, much less where they were going.

Mr. Rubble drummed his fingers on the armrest for several minutes, then turned to Ned. "There's a dirt road that turns off just across the county line. You know the one?" he asked.

Ned took his eyes off the road for a full five seconds as he stared at Mr. Rubble. "What are you getting at?" he asked in a low voice.

Mr. Rubble stared back. "You didn't answer me," he came back sharply. "Do you know where it is?"

Ned hesitated several seconds before answering. "I know where you mean."

The girls alternately looked at Ned and Mr. Rubble as each man spoke. Mr. Rubble's tone of voice had turned deadly serious. Ned's knowing looks said even more.

Moments later Ned slowed down and turned onto a small dirt road. The overhanging trees brushed the top of the truck making loud crashing noises overhead. Finally, Mr. Rubble signaled Ned and he pulled the truck to a stop.

There was complete silence. The men sat still for a moment, then reached for the door handles and stepped out. They walked to the front of the truck. An argument was taking place, but they kept their voices down so neither girl could hear.

The girls froze, their hands locked together as they stared out the front window. Then, Becky turned and looked at Amy Jo. Her eyes asked what her voice was incapable of saying.

It came to her like an answer to a prayer. Amy Jo signaled frantically to Becky. A second later, they flung themselves over the front seat, pulled the  doors shut, and locked them. Amy Jo positioned herself on the edge of the driver's seat just as the men raced back and tried to open the doors.

"Where's first gear?" Amy Jo began frantically. "I've done this a dozen times at the barn." The grinding sound made by the gears being stripped was deafening, but the truck finally shot forward.

Becky sat with her knees on the seat telling Amy Jo which way to turn to keep them on the road. "Turn right, turn right, turn right!" she screamed as the truck nearly ran into a tree.

"I heard you the first time!" Amy Jo yelled back.

The men were running along beside the truck wildly reaching for the locked door handle, shouting promises that fell on deaf ears.

Becky was pounding on the dash board. "Left, left, left, the road turns left!"

Amy Jo pulled the wheel to the left as fast as she could. "Okay, okay!" she shouted back.

The men had jumped onto the running board on each side of the truck. They held onto the door handle with one hand and balled the other into a fist to pound on the windows. Their faces twisted as sweat trickled down their cheeks.

Becky stared out the front window and gasped. "That limb!" she pointed ahead. "Do you think we can go under it?"

"No choice!" Amy Jo decided as they went crashing under it.

Ned hadn't seen it coming.

One down and one to go.

Mr. Rubble stopped pounding for a moment as he regained his balance. He looked behind, but all he could see was a heap on the side of the road struggling to get up.

"How can we get rid of Rubble?" asked Becky, dropping the "Mr."

Amy Jo had a cramp in her leg from straining to reach the pedal. "We can't slam on the brakes or it'll throw Flash and the ponies," she said, her voice nearly normal.

"I know!" Becky was jumping up and down. "You speed up and I'll unlock the door and open it real quick and knock him off the running board."

Amy Jo took her eyes off long enough to stare bug-eyed at her friend who didn't have a mean bone in her body. "Okay, partner, let me pick up some speed and I'll tell you when. She inched forward on the seat and pressed her foot down on the pedal. They shot forward suddenly and Amy Jo shouted. "Now!!"

In one motion Becky yanked up on the lock and shoved the door open.

Mr. Rubble was caught so completely off guard that he flew off the running board and fell to the ground on his back. There he lay, the wind knocked completely out of him.

Amy Jo let up slightly on the pedal as Becky pulled the door shut.

"Yes!" shouted Becky, jumping up so quickly she hit her head on the ceiling.

Amy Jo gaped at her friend again. "What has gotten into you?" she asked.

And then they saw it. Red and white swirling lights just behind them with a screeching siren making beautiful music.

They were safe.

Epilogue

Charlie was a hero, and he wasn't going to let anybody forget it. He liked to brag about how he had found the cell phone in the stall while he was locked up in there. Actually, it was Toby who nosed around in the straw and discovered it. The small object had slipped out of Mr. Rubble's pocket the day before while he was fluffing up the straw.

Freddie had taught Charlie how to dial 911 for emergencies, and that's just what he did. Of course, he neglected to explain that the operator could barely understand him through the tirade of tears. Fortunately, she got enough out of the little fellow to find out where he was. After Officer Higgins raced over to rescue him, Charlie explained about the girls. The officer put out an all-points bulletin, and two policemen arrested Ned and Mr. Rubble before the girls could do them any more damage.

A week later found Charlie and the girls all recovered and at the racetrack. Freddie entered Flash O' Lightning in the maiden race since the three-year-old had never won any races before.

Freddie, Charlie, Amy Jo, and Becky had choice seats in the grandstand with Charlie between the two girls.

The girls positively gawked at everything, especially the horses being paraded in front of them.

"There's Tommy!" squealed Charlie, pointing his finger at Flash's rider. "He's got your colors on, Grandpa. Do you see his green and white jacket and cap?"

Freddie nodded as he nervously patted his grandson's shoulder.

Charlie lifted his head and raised his voice. "We're going to win this race, right, Grandpa?"

Amy Jo and Becky ducked their heads a little. Even though it meant saving the farm if Flash O' Lightning won, they still wished Charlie would pipe down a little bit.

The outrider had mounted his pony and was escorting Flash O' Lightning and Tommy to the starting gate. Post time was only a few minutes away. There was just time to load Flash into his assigned stall in the starting gate.

In the grandstand, the girls sat down and stood up with Charlie alternating their positions. As they sat down, he stood up. It was almost like watching the horses on the merry-go-round at the fair.

The crowd hushed as the last horse was loaded into post position. The bell sounded, the doors flew open, and the announcer cried, "And they're off!"

Ten horses bolted out of the gate as everyone in the grandstand stood up. The distance was seven furlongs with ten horses straining to run the fastest in the seven-eighths of a mile race. As they passed the second furlong, Flash was dead last. Four hearts sunk.

Freddie took his hat off and ran his hand over his head. "Flash is a typical closer," he began. "Stays at the back of the pack until close to the end.  He'll start to pull up to the front soon," he said without conviction.

The girls rung their hands together in mute silence while Charlie shrieked war cries and wildly flung his arms about nearly knocking the girls back into their seats.

Footing from the track was kicked up by the front riders right into Tommy and Flash's face. They were really eating the dirt. Tommy lifted his stick to strike Flash for the first time ever. The jockey was desperate for his horse to make his move. Before Tommy had a chance to bring it down on Flash's back, the colt shot forward and began to close in on the horses in front.

One by one he picked them off as he edged his way to the front. It was as if the horse knew what was at stake. Tommy leaned forward slightly, his arms moved in motion with the colt's strides. The first four horses were picked off one by one.

For two furlongs, Flash rode side by side with two other horses before pulling away. Three more horses to pass and two more furlongs in which to do it. Two of those horses fell behind as Flash overtook them. One more furlong, and one more horse to pass. Flash and the other horse were neck and neck. And with one more stretch, Flash O' Lightning pulled away just enough to pass the finish line first.

Now, up in the grandstand, four sets of arms were flailing and thrashing each other on the back.

Tommy pulled Flash up to a trot to cool him off.

Freddie and Charlie flew out of the grandstand to catch up with Tommy and the winning colt with the girls trailing behind.

"Well," Amy Jo began, "that's one less worry for Freddie."

"Yeah," answered Becky quietly. "Tomorrow Huey comes back, and we can take a breather for awhile."

"I could use a break," Amy Jo admitted.

"Not too long a break," Becky warned.

"Well, I didn't mean a long vacation," Amy Jo countered. "What I meant was I saw this ad in the paper for a job, but it doesn't start for another week."

Becky looked over suspiciously. "What kind of job?"

"You'll love it," Amy Jo promised. "We just have to take care of an old house while the owner is on vacation. You know . . . water plants, bring in the mail, stack the newspapers, stuff like that. Simple enough, no problems, piece of cake."

"Right!" said Becky sarcastically. "Piece of cake? I'll believe it when I see it."